# Paris in the Year 2000

# Paris in the Year 2000

by
**Dr. Tony Moilin**

translated, annotated and introduced by
**Brian Stableford**

A Black Coat Press Book

ISBN 978-1-61227-160-6. First Printing. April 2013. Published by Black Coat Press, an imprint of Hollywood Comics.com, LLC, P.O. Box 17270, Encino, CA 91416. All rights reserved. Except for review purposes, no part of this book may be reproduced or transmitted in any form or by any means, electronic or mechanical, including photocopying, recording, or by any information storage and retrieval system, without permission in writing from the publisher. The stories and characters depicted in this novel are entirely fictional. Printed in the United States of America.

# TABLE OF CONTENTS

# Introduction

*Paris en l'an 2000*, by-lined Docteur Tony Moilin′ (his actual forenames were Julius-Antoine), here translated as *Paris in the Year 2000*, was published in Paris by the author, in association with the Libraire de la Renaissance, in 1869. Moilin had previously published consisted of three medical textbooks, *Leçons de Médecine physiologique* (1866) *Manuel de Médecine physiologique* (1867) and *Traité élémentaire, théorique et pratique du Magnétisme* (1869), and three political pamphlets, *Programme de discussion pour les sociétés populaires* (1868), *La Liquidation sociale* (1869) and *Le Suffrage universel* (1869), but *Paris en l'an 2000* was his first venture into fiction. It was also his last; his career came to an abrupt end not long thereafter.

In August 1870 Moilin was charged with involvement in a plot to assassinate Napoléon III and sentenced to prison for five years. He was liberated during the Prussians' siege of Paris, and enlisted in the National Guard as a surgeon-major, probably under compulsion, as a condition of his release. When the Commune took control of Paris Moilin did not join it, but he agreed to accept the position of Maire of the 6th arrondissement when the Communards attempted to set up an Administration for the city. He was taken prisoner in May when the Commune fell, rapidly court-martialed, ostensibly for having accepted the administrative post, and summarily executed by firing-squad. He was thirty-nine years old; prior to his conviction he had been the assistant of the renowned physician and physiologist Claude

7

Bernard (1813-1876) at the Collège de France, having formerly been his pupil.

Although it would obviously be an exaggeration to say that it was Moilin's publication of *Paris en l'an 2000* that had prompted the authorities to trump up a charge on which to imprison him, and then to put him before a firing squad without even taking the trouble to trump up anything faintly resembling a justification, it was surely a significant factor. It is generally true that although scrupulous accounts of ideal societies tend to bore those readers who are sympathetic to the ideas set out therein, they horrify and terrify readers opposed to them, sometimes arousing an uncommonly violent indignation. By the same token, the various works that reacted against the ideas elaborated in Moilin's utopia— some of whose authors had obviously read it—are much more dramatic and satirically spirited than any work espousing those ideas could possibly hope to be. Such anti-Socialist works as René du Mesnil de Maricourt's *La Commune en l'an 2073: au bout du fossé!* (1874; tr. as "All the Way! The Commune in 2073") and Maurice Spronck's *L'An 330 de la République* (1894; tr. as "Year 330 of the Republic" [1]) are far more flamboyant and rhetorically effervescent, because attack is inherently more glamorous than defense.

Moilin's work never attained anything remotely akin to the success of its most obvious predecessor, Louis-Sébastien Mercier's *L'An deux mille quatre cent quarante* (1771; tr. as *Memoirs of the Year 2500*), or the best-selling socialist utopia of the 19th century, Edward Bellamy's *Looking Backward, 2000-1887* (1888), but it

---

[1] Included in the Black Coat Press collection *Investigations of the Future*, ISBN 978-1-61227-106-4.

would probably have had a wider circulation and attracted more discussion had it not appeared on the eve of the Franco-Prussian War and been so rapidly eclipsed by that catastrophe; the murder of its author cannot have helped, even though its aftermath granted him a kind of martyrdom. Indeed, there is a darkly ironic sense in which the Franco-Prussian War showed up the greatest flaw in the historical schema sketched out in *Paris en l'an 2000*, of which the author was all too obviously painfully aware by the time he recorded it.

In the same way that religious authors who set out painstakingly and analytically to "justify the ways of God to man" in dramatic terms often end up, consciously or unconsciously, in the Devil's party, with their initial faith shattered, shaken or transfigured, writers of utopian novels often reach a point in their own analysis where their own faith falters, and they realize that what they are endeavoring to offer as a viable and practicable political prospectus is, in fact, a mere dream impossible of attainment. That point is usually recognizable because the satirical sarcasm that can never be far below the surface of any hypothetical image of a reconstructed society suddenly breaks free and becomes explosive, causing a fracture from which the text might never recover. *Paris en l'an 2000* provides an unusually clear example of that; once Moilin's sarcasm had grabbed the bit and carried him away in section 3 of Chapter V, it never consented to be thoroughly disciplined again, and the narrative seems to lose a certain amount of heart thereafter, plugging on with a determination that, although far from grim, is a trifle lacking in wholehearted enthusiasm and conviction.

Although Moilin's utopia is set squarely in the euchronian tradition founded by Mercier, it also represents, in one sense, an inversion of the strategy followed by its august predecessor. In order to add new verve to the somewhat tired tradition of utopias set on faraway islands, attained with difficulty by travelers who have usually lost their way, Mercier took the unprecedented step of setting his in the future, in a real place, and representing it as a potential social achievement rather than an intrinsically-remote possibility. Many others followed in his footsteps, some of them going so far as to abandon the visionary framework that Mercier had felt obliged to employ, there being no other way in 1771 to gain seemingly-plausible access to a future viewpoint, although the idea of employing a future-located narrative gradually gained acceptance thereafter simply by courtesy of familiarity. Inevitably, however, as visions of future Paris accumulated in number and variety, the more obvious their contingency became and the greater the tendency became to have fun with their speculative elements, either satirically or simply flamboyantly.

By the 1850s, such visions of future Paris as those contained in Théophile Gautier's "Paris futur" (1851; tr. as "Future Paris" [2]) and Joseph Méry's roughly contemporary "Ce qu'on verra" (original publication untraced; tr. as "What We Shall See" [3]) found it both difficult and undesirable to take themselves too seriously, and a rich tradition of stories sardonically depicting future Paris in ruins, cast into the dustbin of history, its relics misinterpreted by blinkered archeologists, had been launched by Méry's "Les Ruines de Paris" (c1844; tr. as "The Ruins

---

[2] Included in the Black Coat Press collection *Investigations of the Future*, ISBN 978-1-61227-106-4.
[3] Included in the Black Coat Press collection *The Tower of Destony*, ISBN 978-1-61227-101-9.

of Paris" [4]), to be carried forward in striking fashion by Alfred Bonnardot's "Archéopolis" (1857; tr. as "Archeopolis" [5]) and Hippolyte Mettais' *L'An 5865* (1865; tr. as *The Year 5865* [6]). Moilin had probably read some of those works, and might well have been acquainted with Mettais, a fellow-physician also working in Paris. It is, therefore, not entirely surprising that he decided to turn the strategy on its head, by presenting a supposedly futuristic viewpoint that is actually a feint, and describing what is, in effect, an alternative present: a state that might be established by means of purely political action beginning in the present day.

To this end, *Paris en l'an 2000* takes virtually no account of the possibility of technical progress. Although it imagines a very dramatic transformation of the physical appearance of Paris, that metamorphosis is not dependent on any new technological discoveries, except perhaps in terms of the swiftness with which it can allegedly be carried out—and it has to be remembered that Moilin had already been witness to a large-scale transformation of Paris carried out under the auspices of Baron Haussmann, and therefore knew very well what marvels could be accomplished in a relatively short time. Although the extraordinarily elaborate systems of railways and bridges that form an integral part of his imagined Paris would represent an amazing feat of engineering, and the trains traveling on it are radically redesigned, the only significant technological innovation cit-

---

[4] Included in the Black Coat Press collection *The Tower of Destiny*, ISBN 978-1-61227-101-9.
[5] Included in the Black Coat Press collection *Nemoville*, ISBN 978-1-61227-070-8.
[6] Available from Black Coat Press, ISBN 978-1-61227-100-2.

ed is a smoke-absorbing facility fitted to the locomotives.

Indeed, the only item of technology cited in the novella whose means of realization clearly did not exist in 1869 is the one featured in the most far-reaching paragraph of section 3 of chapter V, and it was probably not until he reached that point in his writing that Moilin realized both how crucial that particular innovation might, and how unlikely it was that, even if the relevant discovery did work in the way he imagined, it would have the effect he was compelled to attribute to it.

We now know, of course, what effect the actual equivalent of that particular discovery really did have, just as we know about all the other things detailed in the novella that never happened between 1869 and the year 2000, because we now know exactly what Paris was really like in the year in question. That awareness, however, merely serves to emphasize the fact that *Paris en l'an 2000* ought to be regarded as an alternative history rather than a future history, and enhances its comparative dimension. In his "advertisement" Moilin asks his readers to make their own judgment as to the desirability of the society he describes, but his contemporary readers were not really in a position to make a reasoned judgment on that point, as the present-day Paris that provided their only yardstick was about to be rendered helpless by Prussian guns and then further smashed up, physically as well as politically, by the localized civil war that obliterated the Commune. Modern readers are, therefore, much better situated to make multiple comparisons between Moilin's imaginary Paris, the actual Paris of the year 2000, and a whole host of other hypothetical Parises produced in the interim between 1771 and now.

In 1869, of course, nothing resembling a Socialist Republic had ever existed, and the idea was pristine in its imaginative purity, although a distinct note of skeptical sarcasm with regard to social perfectibility in general had crept into Moilin's hypothetical construction even before he reached the fatal fault-line—a note particularly plangent in section 6 of chapter III. The situation is very different today. Many ostensible Socialist Republics have been established—fleetingly, for the most part—and, far from being pristine, the whole notion now seems irredeemably tarnished by mostly-bitter historical experience. Beneath the stains inflicted upon it, however, the idea itself retains a fugitive innocence, enshrining the hopeful ideal that motivated Tony Moilin and formulated his endeavor. It is not insignificant that France is one European nation where that ideal still retains some muscle and vigor, and where it continues to surface—even, on occasion, although compromised in every imaginable way, in elections for the Presidency of the Republic. Some credit for that retained vigor is due to the impetus lent to it along its long and thorny path by the likes of Louis-Sébastien Mercier and Tony Moilin, as well as to the historical examples of the 1789 Revolution and the Commune.

Tony Moilin is the only martyr of the Commune who is granted a forename as well as a surname in the best-known commemorative protest song that emerged from the aftermath of its suppression, *Elle n'est pas morte!* [It (i.e., the Commune) is not Dead!] (1886), written by Eugène Pottier, who also wrote the words to the *Internationale*, to be sung to a familiar tune by Victor Parizot. That exception has more to do with preserving the scansion of the relevant verse than Moilin's perceived historical importance, but it is still a tribute of sorts. Wikipedia lists twelve versions of the song in question recorded between 1967 and 2008, so the worthy doctor's name is unlikely to fall into total oblivion any time soon, even without the assistance of this translation.

One further preservation of Moilin's name, and the contents of *Paris en l'an 2000* in particular, that is worthy of mention is the novella's citation in Walter Benjamin's *Das Passangen-Werk* (tr. 2002 as *The Arcades Project*), a work that Benjamin began in 1927 and left incomplete on his death in 1940, and which he intended to be his magnum opus. When the existing text was edited and published in the 1980s it attracted a great deal of attention and controversy, and Benjamin's account of Moilin's "gallery-streets," as an important adjunct to the evolution of the arcades of Paris and the culture they helped to create and shape, has helped to renew interest in *Paris en l'an 2000*. That particular innovation, sociological rather than technological, along with the consequences that Moilin attributes to it, does, indeed, constitute the most original and fascinating aspect of the novella, all the more so because it is largely independent of the work's political propaganda.

The translation has been made from the version of the first edition reproduced on the Bibliothèque Nationale's *gallica* website.

Brian Stableford

# PARIS IN THE YEAR 2000

## *ADVERTISEMENT*

I confess that the Paris that is in question in this work bears little resemblance to present-day Paris. To all the incredulous individuals who find my reforms too radical and impossible to realize, I will only say one thing in reply: that between now and then, 131 years will go by, and during that long lapse of time, more than one revolution might occur, and bring about many changes.

There is, however, one thing that will not change so soon; that is the very foundation of human nature, and for a long time yet, people will be egotistical and sensual. That is why, unlike some other Socialists, I have abstained from crediting all qualities and all virtues to the inhabitants of my ideal Republic. They are human beings, neither better nor worse than those of today; sometimes, by design, I have even exaggerated their faults, so fearful was I of falling into the ridiculous utopia of universal perfection.

All the reforms that I have indicated, therefore, have taken place not in human beings themselves but in the institutions that rule them. To put them into practice, it would not be necessary to wait for citizens to be more enlightened, more virtuous and more disinterested that they are at present; it would be sufficient to make a few new laws and repeal a few others, and the social Republic would function with the French people of the present day as well as with those of the future.

Throughout the course of my book, I have supposed that we are living in the year 2000 and that my reforms, already accepted for a long time, have borne all their fruit. That is a literary procedure intended to give ideas a more gripping form and set the things themselves before the eyes. In comparing the Society of the year 2000 with that of today, readers will easily be able to see the difference, and choose which of the two seems preferable to them.

But when, I might be asked, will the social renovation that I propose take place? Will it not be for another century, or in an era much closer to the present? That is a question that it is not up to me to decide, and which must be settled by the Parisians themselves, since it concerns the city that they inhabit. It is for them to decide whether they are satisfied with their present situation, or whether, on the contrary, they desire a change, and are resolved to do what is necessary to obtain it.

# I. THE TRANSFORMATION OF PARIS

## 1. The Expropriation of Houses

When the Socialists came to power and were the masters of Paris, the first thing they had to think about was expropriating the houses of the city, in order to transform them and bring them into line with the new social institutions.

The architects consulted in this regard wanted everything to be demolished, and then to have "model houses" constructed, at great expense, in conformity with the plans they presented. Fortunately, the Government was as prudent as it was economical. It therefore rejected the architects' projects, which would have involved too great an expense, preferring to utilize the houses of Paris as they were and to adapt them as well as possible to their new purpose, rather than launch into a costly system of demolition and reconstruction.

Before giving the details of that transformation of the capital, however, let us first explain how the Administration went about expropriating all the houses in Paris and becoming their legitimate owner. That acquisition of an entire city was all the more remarkable as a financial operation because the State, when the Republic was inaugurated, had debts of more than eighty billion and not a centime in its coffers.

Far from being alarmed by that penury, and knowing perfectly well that France was rich enough to pay its old debts and to contract new ones, the Government, as soon as it as solidly established, hastened to expropriate all the houses in Paris, paying a fair price to their owners. They did not make that payment in metallic money, since they did not have any. Nor did they make it in paper money that would have been immediately depreciated, and rightly refused by the owners. They did it quite simply, and to general satisfaction, with entitlements to annual income payable by the public Treasury.

The mean income of each house was calculated in accordance with the rents of the previous fifty years, and then that income was capitalized, at a standard interest of 5%. The capital thus calculated was transformed into yearly income in conformity with the tariffs adopted by the Insurance Companies.

In the early days it was necessary to give very large sums to the former owners, but as they were dying every day, the income paid to them diminished every year, and was soon amply covered by the produce of the rents paid by the citizens to the State.

Furthermore, what greatly aided the Socialist Government to pay off its own debts and those of previous regimes was the introduction of an income tax.

This new tax was based in the following manner. It was proportional to income so long as that did not exceeded 12,000 francs per year, but above that figure it became total—which is to say that it confiscated, purely and simply, everything in excess of the regulation sum of 12,000 francs. The Government considered that that maximum income would be amply sufficient to procure all the well-being desirable to its fortunate possessor, and that tolerating fortunes of twenty, fifty, a hundred or two hundred thousand francs of income, and even more, was encouraging idleness and bad habits, and conserving the worst abuses of the old regime.

When, therefore, one of these individuals was expropriated who had a large income from houses—a hundred thousand francs, for example—the Treasury expropriation duly gave him an annual entitlement proportional to his former fortune, but when it was a matter of drawing that income, the collector of income tax similarly performed his function. Of the hundred thousand francs, he took 88,000 for the State and only left 12,000 to the expropriated individual.

The latter certainly made some complaint on seeing himself thus reduced to the adequate portion, but as the tax in question had been voted by the Representatives of the country and the Administration saw to its strict execution, there was no objection to be raised and, whether he liked it or not, he had to submit to the law.

## 2. Gallery-Streets

As soon as the Socialist Government had become the legitimate owner of all the houses in Paris, it handed them over to the architects, with orders to get the best out of them, and especially to establish the *gallery-streets* indispensable to the new Society.

The architects carried out the mission entrusted to them as best they could.

On the first floor of each house they took over all the rooms overlooking the street and demolished the intermediary partitions; then they opened large bays in the party walls and thus obtained gallery-streets that had the height and width of an ordinary room and occupied the entire length of a block of buildings.

In the newer quarters, where the contiguous houses have floors at very nearly the same height, the floors of the galleries were sufficiently level, and only small adjustments had to be made. In the old streets, however, things were different. There, it was necessary to raise or lower many floors, and it was often necessary to settle for giving the resultant floor a marked slope or interrupting it with a few flights of steps.

When all the blocks of houses were thus pierced by galleries occupying the length of their first floor, there was no more to do than connect these separate fragments together and thus form an uninterrupted network embracing the entire extent of the city. This was easily accomplished by establishing covered bridges on each street that had the same height and width as the galleries and were fused with them.

Similar bridges, but much longer, were even extended over the various boulevards, over the squares and over the bridges crossing the Seine, so that the gallery-street did not suffer any break in continuity. A pedestrian could thus travel throughout the city without ever being exposed, and, in consequence, was always perfectly sheltered from the rain or the sun.

Furthermore, all these works were carried out with the feverish rapidity to which Revolutions give birth; the laborers worked on them night and day. After a few weeks, the transformation of Paris was complete, and people began to appreciate the results.

As soon as Parisians had experienced the new galleries, they no longer wanted to set foot in the old streets, which, they said, were now only good for dogs. When anyone suggested that they might go outside, they always found that it was too hot or too cold, that there was mud, fog, wind or dust, and they preferred to remain under cover.

Far from suffering, their health only improved, and the almost complete disappearance was observed of all the maladies caused by cold or damp, such as colds, rheumatism, neuralgia, pulmonary fluxions and so on. Moreover, they made considerable savings on clothing and footwear. Their garments, no longer being damaged by rain and dirt, did not wear out nearly as rapidly, and maintained their freshness longer—not to mention that people were liberated from all the costly devices invented as protection again rain, cold and the sun, such as umbrellas, parasols, mufflers, mantles, rubber boots and so on.

Everyone, therefore, was satisfied, except for a few malcontents, of whom there are always some, who can never constrain themselves from criticizing the government and opposing it.

On the one hand, there were all the shopkeepers, who lamented in chorus that their customers had been taken away. No one any longer passed in front of their shops; they would no longer be able to sell anything and bankruptcy was certain. On the other hand, a considerable number of inhabitants complained that their industry had been greatly compromised or even entirely obliterated.

There were manufacturers of umbrellas, and parasols, and those of rubber clothing or footwear, who could no longer sell their merchandise. There were shops selling clothing and lingerie, tailors, hat-makers, cobblers, hair-dressers and couturiers who could no longer cover their expenses, because the articles they provided did not have to be renewed as frequently once they were no longer dampened by rain, dirtied by mud or burned by the sun. There were coachmen and entrepreneurs of public transport who were about to lose all the clients that rainy days attracted to them. Finally, there were physicians, surgeons and pharmacists, who would no longer have sick people to treat once the public ceased to breathe damp air, get their feet wet, catch colds, slip on black ice and get run over by carriages.

There were many other similar and no less self-interested complaints, but the Government remained unmoved by them and, confident in the ultimate result of its efforts, it continued resolutely with the work of transformation that it had begun.

## 3. Model Houses

However, the architects to whom the houses of Paris had been handed over did not stop at opening up the gallery-streets that we have described, but passed on to the upper floors. There too they pierced the party walls and put all the habitations in communication.

That new circulation did not take place in gallery-streets, of course, which would have wasted too much space, but it was facilitated by variously obscure narrow and winding corridors. Thanks to these corridors, which circulated throughout a block of houses, one could reach any part of the neighborhood in a matter of minutes without taking a single unnecessary step and, so to speak, without leaving home. Little footbridges extended over the streets linked the corridors of the upper floors together, and formed a new system of communication that embraced all the houses of the same quarters within its network, and was only interrupted by the quais and the boulevards. These little passages were immediately found to be very convenient, and the inhabitants did not neglect to make use of them in order to visit neighbors or when they went out in casual clothing.

When the architects had finished all these piercings and found themselves without work they began to pursue the Government with their plans for *model houses*, and, as the public Treasury had abundant funds, thanks to the returns of the income tax, it was not very difficult for them to obtain commissions for the projects they were requesting.

All the old, badly-constructed, badly-ventilated and poorly-distributed houses were therefore demolished, and in their place, model dwellings were built, disposed in the following manner:

Every new construction formed a large square whose center was empty and was occupied by courtyards and gardens. The basements, very spacious and well-lit, were all in communication; they formed long galleries that followed the trajectories of the streets, where an underground railway was established. That railway was not intended for passengers, but only for cumbersome merchandise—wine, wood, coal, etc.—which it transported all the way to the interior of houses. Vast storage facilities situated alongside the track served to receive all the products that were not endangered by damp.

Finally, these subterranean levels also contained conduits for water and gas, air-tubes for the postal service, and immense mobile barrels that replaced the old cesspits, and which the railway carried away as soon as they were full. As new constructions gradually replaced the old, these subterranean railways acquired an increasing importance, and did not take long to form complete networks serving entire quarters.

The ground floor of a model house is divided into large well-ventilated and well-lit rooms. These mostly do not serve as dwellings, but as workshops for various industries or as large warehouses for all kinds of merchandise that need to be kept dry.

The first floor in occupied by gallery-streets of unequal dimensions. Along the major roads, they take up the entire length of the building and are proportionately high. Magnificently furnished and decorated, they form "salon-streets," whose description can be read further on. Other galleries, much less spacious, are more moderately decorated. They are reserved for commercial retailers, who display their merchandise there in such a way that passers by no longer circulate past shops but through them, thus being more keenly tempted by the objects placed before their eyes.

On the upper floors the model houses are divided into a multitude of rooms of various sizes, all illuminated, some overlooking the street and others the courtyard. All of them open into a central corridor that runs the entire length of the building. At its two extremities that corridor ends in monumental staircases that occupy the four corners of the edifice and establish a broad communication between the floors. In addition, for the convenience of the inhabitants, in the middle of each corridor one finds a small spiral staircase that leads rapidly between floors and dispenses with the need to go the long way round via the large corner stairways. Finally, a mechanical elevator, which goes all the way down to the cellars, permits furniture, fuel and packages to be lifted to any floor, for the benefit of people who live on higher levels and do not like to tire themselves out.

Model houses thus rise up to a height of ten stories. The architects proposed to take that number to fifteen, or even to eighteen, in order to obtain greater economies in the cost of construction, but the Government did not adopt those proposals, which would have caused citizens to live at too great a height and oblige them to make overly difficult ascents.

Finally, let us not forget to mention that all the model dwellings are linked together, and to the old houses, by large covered bridges and numerous footbridges, which permit circulation in all directions and at the height of every floor.

While being actively occupied in transforming Paris, however, the Government of the Social Republic did not neglect the provinces. In all cities, even those of the limited size, it expropriated private houses, pierced gallery-streets and constructed model houses, always remembering that, although the mind of France is centralized in Paris, the activity of Paris has to spread out and make itself felt throughout the rest of France.

### 4. The International Palace

The Palace in question is the most magnificent monument every constructed by humans, and when foreigners come to Paris it is the first thing that they ask to visit, so great is the universal celebrity of that marvelous edifice.

The International Palace occupies, all by itself, the entire surface of the Cité and the Île Saint-Louis, which have been cleared and then joined together by filling in the arm of the Seine that separated them. Seen as a whole, it presents the form of an immense, perfectly regular ship whose prow is the tip of the Île Saint-Louis and whose poop in the platform of the Pont Neuf, and which rises from the middle of the river as if emerging from the bosom of the waves.

To the south and north, the two facades of an immense development are constituted by three stages of terraces and columns, which occupy the entire length of the two islands and form three galleries extending as far as the eye can see, whose appearance could not be any more grandiose, and which strike all spectators with profound admiration.

The first of these colonnades, the highest of them, dips its feet in the Seine, so to speak, and overlooks the summits of the neighboring houses. Often inundated when big floods occur, it offers a very pleasant promenade during the heat-waves of summer, and then becomes the favorite rendezvous of Parisian sailors and anglers.

Above that first construction is a large balcony and a second gallery, from which the panorama of Paris and the surrounding countryside can be seen unfurling at one's feet.

Finally, on that second colonnade, a third had been built, whose boldness all architects admire, and which gives the edifice a singularly monumental aspect. It supports a vast terrace bordered by a perforated balustrade, which looks from below like lace but takes on gigantic proportions at close range.

The eastern and western facades of the Palace, much less developed than the preceding ones, similarly present a triple row of galleries, except that these are not in a straight line but describe a rounded vault. They are also ornamented with statues and bas-reliefs, and in their disposition they resemble the prow and poop of a stone vessel floating on the Seine, encompassing within its vast hull the entire area that the primitive Paris of the Gauls and the Romans once occupied.

The interior façade of the Palace is no less magnificent than the one overlooking the river, but it is constructed in a less severe style, and a gracious ornamentation breaks up the monotony of its lines in a pleasant manner.

The International Palace serves as the residence of the Government of the Social Republic. To that effect, it is divided up into halls, galleries, offices and other rooms designed for public services, furnished and decorated with sumptuous magnificence. The most curious part of the Palace, however—the one that visitors want to visit first—is the Temple of the socialist religion, a magnificent edifice that surpasses in its grandeur and richness the most beautiful cathedrals of other religions.

Situated in the middle of the two conjoined islands, in the same place that Notre-Dame once occupied, the Temple is itself a monument, forming an integral part of another monument, which it overlooks and overwhelms. On its rounded flanks, a thousand monstrous columns rise up above the mass of the Palace, seemingly intent on scaling the sky and raising into the clouds an immense, unprecedented, prodigious dome, the iron employed in its construction having rendered all the audacities of architecture possible and, so to speak, having realized the dream of the Tower of Babel.

Inside, the socialist Temple forms a nave unique in the world, of an incredible extent and elevation, which sustains on either side a double row of colossal pillars. No one who has not seen that spectacle could ever imagine the powerful and grandiose effect of those gigantic pillars, which launch themselves in a single jet from the ground to the cupola, and which, by a clever effect of perspective, seem to be even taller than they really are.

The aisles of the Temple, constructed in less majestic proportions more in accord with human smallness, are, by contrast, ornamented with an extraordinary magnificence and seek to flatter the eye that they cannot astonish. The most brilliant marbles, which further emphasize the severity of the bronzes and the gleam of the gold, serves as frames for paintings, status and bas-reliefs, while a mysterious light filtered by stained-glass windows plays over all those fine things and animates them with magical reflections.

It is in these aisles—which, if they were isolated, would constitute vast temples in themselves—that all the ceremonies of the socialist religion take place: ceremonies as simple in their initial conception as they are magnificent in their execution, and in which is found the objective of the endeavor.

## 5. Metropolitan Railways

It was not enough for the Socialist Government to create circulation inside houses; it was also necessary to organize it in the old streets, and endow the city with a system of railways permitting rapid transport from one place to another.

To that effect, it began by constructing twenty railways that all departed from the center of Paris, from the International Palace, and headed toward the capital's various barriers, where they linked up with the provincial lines.

These radial railways occupy the middle of broad boulevards recently-pierced and bordered with model houses. They are established on rather high viaducts, which pass over streets, and consequently do not impede the movement of vehicles and pedestrians in any way. These viaducts, constructed entirely in iron and with long spans, are astonishing in their lightness and resilience, and, far from injuring the beauty of the city, form one of its principal ornaments.

Nothing is as magnificent as the sight of these aerial railways, several kilometers long, which, borne by their countless arches, describe interminable straight lines disappearing over the horizon. It is, most of all, from the top of the International Palace that the spectacle is grandiose. The twenty viaducts arriving, so to speak, from all the countries of the world, carrying the passengers of the Two Worlds on their rails, come to end at our feet, thus providing the most griping image of the universal fraternity of peoples and the unity of the human race.

The system of metropolitan railways is completed by a second network, which follows circular courses. These further tracks are established on lower viaducts, which pass underneath the radial lines. They all depart from the Seine and form half a dozen equally-spaced circling railways around the International Palace, serving all the quarters of the city.

Numerous trains pulled by smoke-absorbing locomotives circulate at brief intervals on all the metropolitan railways. These trains travel at quite rapid speeds, and yet they frequently pick up and set down passengers *en route*, thanks to a very ingenious system which, at each station, permits the exchange of the last carriage of the train, without there being any need to stop the latter or even slow it down. Everywhere that a radial railway crosses a circular track, a communal station is established, which permits travel from any quarter to all the others, with the aid of a near-direct trajectory and a single change of train.

The carriages employed by the railways of Paris are large, comfortable, well-ventilated in summer and heated in winter. They are disposed in such a fashion that people can pass from one carriage to another and circulate along the entire length of the train. One boards a train, not by means of lateral doors, but by a unique entrance situated at the rear. At each station, the people who want

29

to get off go into the rearmost carriage, which is discon-
nected and replaced by the carriage in which passengers
joining the train are located.

Metropolitan carriages are of two types. Some, very
simple, provided with solid benches and running no risk
of being damaged, always occupy the rear of the train.
They are designed for ill-clad individuals or those carrying large parcels. The other carriages, placed at the front,
are much more luxurious. Suspended on four springs,
upholstered in rich fabrics, ornamented with trimmings
and softly furnished, they receive all the passengers
whose costumes are in harmony with that sumptuous-
ness. However, the price of these luxurious carriages is
no higher than that of the others, and any individual who
is dressed in a manner not liable to cause any deteriora-
tion is at liberty to go into them.

The price of tickets is very modest—only ten centimes, regardless of the distance traveled. As one can go
anywhere by making a single connection, even the long-
est journey never costs more than twenty centimes. For a
further five centimes, you can board the little omnibuses
that wait at every station and conduct you rapidly to the
very place to which you want to go.

The railways that have just been described are designed exclusively for passengers. As for merchandise,
that circulates via the subterranean railways established
in the basements of model houses—railways that ramify
throughout the interior of Paris and on which a truly incredible volume of transportation takes place.

Thanks to that double circulation of trains, one aerial and the other subterranean, not a single collision oc-
curs, and the city is furrowed night and day in every direction by countless trains, which pass at high speed be-

side or above one another, and cross paths perpetually, without ever being able to crash into one another.

Paris is not the only city to have been endowed with railways; similar systems were established in all the larger cities of the provinces situated on a major route. The networks there are, of course, much less complicated than the one in the capital, reduced to one or two lines serving the station and the principal quarters, designed to transport both goods and passengers.

## 6. The Aspect of the Gallery-Streets

As soon as the gallery-streets had been pierced, the Government took care to decorate them and to bring them into harmony with their various functions.

The broadest and best-situated among them were decorated tastefully and furnished sumptuously. The walls and ceilings were covered with decorative paint, rare marble, gilt, bas-reliefs, mirrors and pictures. The windows were fitted with magnificent hangings and curtains embroidered with marvelous designs; chairs, armchairs and decorative sofas, perfectly stuffed and covered with rich fabrics, offered comfortable seats to weary pedestrians. Finally, artistic items of furniture—antique dressers, sideboards, shelves covered with works of art, statues in marble and bronze, vases containing natural flowers, aquaria filled with live fish and aviaries populated by rare birds—completed the decoration of those gallery-streets, which are illuminated after dusk by thousands of gilded candelabras and crystal chandeliers.

The Government wanted the streets belonging to the people of Paris to surpass in magnificence the reception-rooms of the most powerful sovereigns, and artists, to whom they had given carte blanche, ingeniously gathering all the splendors of civilization in a restricted space, realized marvels in which the most unexpected richness was always allied with elegance and good taste.

As for the gallery-streets that were less favorably situated, they were decorated and furnished much more modestly. The majority of them were devoted to commerce and transformed into retail establishments. Everywhere, their walls were covered by the varied display of all the products of industry. This resulted in a kind of decoration that, although not as opulent as that of the salon-streets, nevertheless charmed the eye, and, thanks to its daily renewal, never wearied the curiosity of passers-by. By virtue of this utilitarian employment of galleries, pedestrians circulated continually in the midst of shops and, without deviating from their route, could buy all the objects that tempted them and of which they had need.

In the early morning, the gallery-streets are surrendered to service personnel, who let in air, carefully sweep, dust, wipe and polish all the furniture, maintaining the most scrupulous tidiness everywhere. Afterwards, according to the season, the windows are either closed or left open, fires are lit or blinds drawn, in order to have a mild and even temperature at all times. For their part, the shop-managers clean up their premises, get out their merchandise, arrange their displays and prepare to receive visits from the public.

Between nine and ten o'clock all the cleaning work is completed and the passers-by, previously sparse, begin to circulate in greater numbers. Entry to the galleries is strictly forbidden to any person who is dirty or carrying large burdens; it is also forbidden to smoke there or to spit. There is rarely any need to remind people of these prohibitions, however; everyone understands that the streets, which are, in essence, fine shops and magnificent salons, would deteriorate very rapidly if people were permitted to spit everywhere and sit down on silk furniture in damp or soiled clothing.

In the afternoon, the crowds become larger and women in elegant costumes begin to appear. Everywhere, there is nothing to be seen but hurried individuals going about their urgent business, buyers examining the displays of shops and asking to inspect merchandise, and inquisitive individuals standing in front of paintings and taking inventory of the myriad curiosities accumulated in showcases—with which no idler, however experienced, can boast of being fully acquainted, and in which, when passing the same places, one always discovers new details that had escaped previous examinations, reawakening a curiosity always satisfied and never sated.

But it is in the evenings, above all, that the gallery-streets present an extraordinary animation, of which no description can give even an approximate idea. The entire population that is working by day in factories, offices and shops, comes together in the gallery-streets, especially in the salon-streets lighted *à giorno* by thousands of chandeliers.

All the women who are still young and pretty stroll there in ball-gowns and satin slippers, their heads decked in flowers, their arms and shoulders bare. They claim that that kind of costume is extremely economical and costs them less than any other form of dress. Their cavaliers are also in very gracious evening suits, which have nothing in common with the cramped frock-coats and stovepipe hats of the old regime. As for old and unpretentious people, their costume is simpler without constituting a stain in the midst of that elegant society.

The evening is thus spent strolling in the street, chatting and laughing with one another about the countless curiosities displayed before the eyes, unless one prefers to go to the theater, a café, a concert-hall or some other place of pleasure.

As the night advances, however, the strollers becomes rarer; everyone goes home; at midnight, the chandeliers are extinguished, save for a few conserved gas-jets, and the only citizens to be seen are those emerging from spectacles and returning to their homes, where they go to sleep with the consciousness that the Social Republic is the best of governments.

# II. THE ORGANIZATION OF LABOR

## *1. Industry*

How to organize workers, to ensure each of them a job and a fair wage: such was the problem that the Funders of the Social Republic had the glory of posing and resolving. By virtue of their concern, Industry, Commerce, Agriculture, Salaries and Unemployment were the object of important decrees that substituted a better state of affairs for the old order of things and became the fundamental charter of the new Society.

With regard to Industry, while leaving scope for individual initiative, it was necessary to furnish instruments of labor and give it all the facilities desirable for the purchase of its raw materials, the sale of its products and the improvement of its equipment.

This is what the Government did.

On the one hand, it organized Commerce (see the following section) and thus made all raw materials available at an extremely low price, simultaneously ensuring manufacturers numerous and regular orders and prompt payment for their work.

On the other hand, it organized Credit and founded a National Bank, whose mission was to lend to Industry and Agriculture and thus favor the development of public wealth.

This National Bank occupies the same site as the old Banque de France. It is one of the most important institutions of the Social Republic. It is designed to lend money to all the manufacturers who need it, and anyone, rich or poor, can obtain credit from it. Thus, any worker who wants to work for himself, any associations of workers that wants to set up a business, and any employer who wants to improve his equipment and increase his production, can obtain aid and protection from the Government, and has only to apply to the National Bank to obtain the necessary loans.

The Bank, of course, does not give its money to just anyone, and only lends its funds to those who present a material or moral guarantee of reimbursement. In fact, the sums advanced by the bank belong to the Nation and are merely a deposit confided to the Government. Now, if the latter lent money to everyone, without doing any research, it would often not be repaid and would be rightly accused of squandering public wealth and mismanaging the country's affairs.

The loans made by the Bank bring in a monthly interest, which is not very considerable, not being at all usurious while nevertheless constituting an important resource for the Treasury. All the sums formerly appropriated by bankers, shareholders, usurers and credit brokers now go into the Nation's coffers, which employs the to pay for public expenses.

Not only does the National Bank advance money to all honest workers and manufacturers, but—in which respect it differs from all the banks of the old regime—it never asks to be reimbursed so long as the interest on the sums advanced is paid regularly. The manufacturer who borrows money can therefore invest in necessary expenses—for example, buying a machine or erecting a building. The State will give him all the time necessary to pay off the debt, and no one will come, after three months, to demand a capital that he can no longer return because the capital no longer exists, having been transformed into an instrument of labor.

*Heavy Industry.*

Heavy industry is that which requires the collaboration of numerous workers and cannot be undertaken appropriately without the employment of a great deal of equipment and considerable capital. Examples are building railways, the transport of goods, the fitting out of ships, mines, quarries, blast-furnaces, gas-plants, refineries, mills, etc.—in a word, all the establishments in which anything is manufactured on a large scale and in which costly machinery is employed, operated by numerous workers.

In the Social Republic, all of this heavy industry has been taken out of private hands, and it is the State that takes charge of managing it and furnishing it with the necessary capital. When the Socialists came to power, the majority of these large industrial establishments were already exploited with the aid of simple employees appointed and paid by Companies of shareholders. More often than not, therefore, the Government only had to let things remain as they were, and merely substitute itself for the shareholders that were expropriated and paid in annual incomes. In the same way as for the houses of Paris, that expropriation was very fruitful for the Treasury, thanks to the income tax that reduced excessively large fortunes to honest proportions and pitilessly raked off everything that exceeded the maximum of twelve thousand francs.

That expropriation of industrial Companies had another advantage, almost as great. That was cutting short all the markets and all the speculations that were made on the shares of Companies as on other stocks. In the last years of the old regime that speculation in shares had attained incredible proportions; it had become a frightful gambling game of ups and downs, an essentially immoral and disastrous game that enriched a few tricksters while ruining a multitude of poor dupes.

The Government hastened to put an end to all that shady dealing. The Bourse, the principal location of the shameful traffic in stocks and shares, was closed and demolished. In its place a square was constructed in which a stream could be seen running over a gilded bed, seemingly flowing with liquid gold, although it was only clear water—a faithful image of all the speculations that had ruined so many gamblers by offering them the hope of a chimerical fortune.

When the Administration took charge of managing heavy industry, many people believed that it was taking on a task that was too burdensome and that it would be impossible to have such complex and considerable interests run by employees. They predicted that Industry and Commerce would immediately come to a halt, and that within a fortnight, France would be prey to the most frightful poverty. The former speculators at the Bourse were particularly inconsolable. Since they could no longer bet on its ups and downs, they were seen everywhere crying that it was the end of civilization and that humankind, approaching its imminent doom, was about to fall back into primitive barbarity.

That sinister prediction was not realized. Far from it; never had France been so rich and prosperous than it has been since the day when the Government put itself at the head of national labor and imprinted it with a vigorous impulsion. By virtue of its care, roads, canals and railways have been constructed in regions that still lacked them; the price of transport by land and sea has been considerably diminished for both goods and passengers. Far from collapsing in the hands of the Administration, all the mines, construction yards and factories have grown considerably under its direction, and deliver their various products in larger quantities and at lower prices than before. Finally, all the workers employed by the State earn their living comfortably; all those who work for themselves or for small manufacturers similarly participate in the general prosperity, and far from cursing the Social Republic, are all ready to shed their blood to defend it.

## 2. Commerce

Among the Republicans of the year 2000, Commerce is strictly forbidden to private individuals, and it is the Government that takes charge of selling, by way of its employees, all the products of light industry and all those that emerge from its own establishments.

Mention has already been made of the wholesale and retails storage facilities installed on the ground floor and in the gallery-streets of model houses. All these shops are run by employees of the State and the considerable profits that result from sales go into the Treasury and are directed to public expenditure.

Let us note here that in the Socialist State, the Government handles all commerce and sells everything, but, except for the products of the national factories, it does not manufacture anything itself, leaving that care to individual initiative. Thus, to cite one example, in a restaurant, the employees paid wages by the State are limited to serving the public and keeping the till and the books, but the restaurateur—which is to say, the person who provisions and supervises the kitchen, is not an employee but a manufacturer in his own right, and quite independent, from whom the Administration buys his products in order to sell them to consumers.

It is the same for all other kinds of commerce; the State sells bread, wine, vegetables, clothes, ironmongery, etc., but it does not manufacture any of these things and always limits itself to serving as an intermediary between the customer and the producer. Selling a product made by someone else is not very difficult; waged employees can easily be charged with that task and carry it out very adequately.

As soon as the Authority had made known its intention to suppress the liberty of Commerce, however, and direct all sales through its employees, a formidable clamor rose up among businessmen and shopkeepers. They said that the liberty of transactions was absolutely indispensable to the prosperity of France and that to allow everything to be sold by the State would be to deliver the country to the corrosive canker of functionarism and bring down terrible catastrophes upon the Nation. Furthermore, they signed an extremely threatening collective petition in which they claimed the liberty of Commerce very energetically, and declared themselves ready to do anything if it were not granted to them.

On reading this petition, the Socialist Government was very perplexed and was wondering anxiously how it would be able to disarm that formidable opposition, when, that same evening, fortunately, it received a multitude of letters that reassured it completely. They were from signatories of the petition, expressing their regret at having signed it; they affirmed that their signatures had been obtained by surprise in a moment of unreflective enthusiasm, and they all concluded their epistles by requesting to be included in the ranks of the State employees responsible in future for carrying out all sales.

Very glad to have got away with it so cheaply, the Government met the majority of those requests favorably and assumed the duty of organizing Commerce.

It began by expropriating the merchandise of the former businessmen, who were reimbursed with annual incomes; then, all the retail establishments were installed in the gallery-streets that had just been pierced, while ground floors were reserved for wholesalers. Naturally, all these shops were divided equitably between the various quarters, and care was taken to maintain a strict proportion between supply and demand, in order to avoid any over-employment.

Remarkably enough—which proved all the advantages of the system of organization—ten new well-provisioned shops were able replace more than five hundred smaller ones, and the customers, far from being injured by that centralization of sales, acquired a greater variety of stock therein and, more importantly, a considerable reduction in prices.

Selling everything in immense quantities, the Administration was content with a small profit on each item of between three and five per cent, and that slender profit not only covered all expenses by brought in enormous sums every year and thus became the most productive and least burdensome of taxes. So, of all the socialist reforms, the one that put Commerce in the hands of the State was one of the most fecund, and immediately realized the low cost of living that so many Governments have promised the People without ever being able to deliver it.

## 3. Agriculture

While occupying itself with the cities, the Government did not forget the rural areas, and too all appropriate measures to encourage the development of Agriculture.

The first and most important of these measures was to give the land to those who cultivated it and to suppress the entire class of landowners who rented their land to others instead of exploiting it themselves.

Here again the Government proceeded in the customary manner, by expropriation. All the lands that had been rented for farming or husbandry were bought by the state and paid for in annual income and were then assigned to the credit of the peasants, with the provision that, in future, each of them would be obliged to cultivate his land himself or sell it to someone else.

In all the terrains of so-called large-scale cultivation, however, where agriculture had something of the industrial about it, the Administration retained possession of the lands it had expropriated and leased them on a long-term basis to intelligent farmers who earned a good living therefrom while paying a substantial rent to the State.

Similarly, the Government retained property in all the forests, as in all the heath-land that seemed appropriate for reforestation. Woods were recognized as indispensable to prevent floods; it was in the highest interests of the State to retain possession of them. Moreover, far from suffering, forestry exploitation had never been as intelligent and advantageous; thanks to the Administration's zeal, immense areas previously abandoned were soon seen covered in plantations that would eventually become vast forests.

The general expropriation of all the farmland had the most fortunate consequences for France. To begin with, it brought a great deal of money into the Treasury, because, of course, the income tax functioned as usual and mercilessly consumed all the allotted incomes that surpassed twelve thousand francs. On the other hand, as soon as the land was in the possession of those who cultivated it, its fecundity was multiplied tenfold; it furnished massive supplies of agricultural foodstuffs to the populations of the cities, which, for their part, inundated rural areas with manufactured goods. From that mutual exchange emerged abundance and wellbeing for everyone, and the peasants, appreciating all the benefits of Socialism, became its most ardent defenders.

But it was not enough to put the land in the hands of cultivators; it was also necessary to give them the means of developing it.

The National Bank provided that. Every peasant who wanted to clear ground, drain it, build, buy feed, animals or agricultural equipment, was able to borrow money on a long-term basis—the only kind of loan appropriate to agriculture. The Bank never reclaimed reimbursement of its advances from anyone who paid the interest regularly. The cultivator, liberated from his hereditary enemies, lack of money and usury, could therefore carry out all the desirable improvements and renounce the spirit of routine that had previously held Agriculture back for so long.

In sum, rural areas profited greatly from all the reforms carried out by the Socialists. New railways, canals and roads, lowering the costs of transportation, facilitated the movement of agricultural produce and rendered their sale easier. On the other hand, since Commerce was organized, the countryman went to the city, and bought all the manufactured goods he needed at a low price there, while he sold his merchandise much more cheaply than before. Thanks to the suppression of courtiers, speculators and all unnecessary intermediaries, agricultural products reached the hands of the consumer directly, and although the latter got them at a much better price than previously, that low price rewarded the cultivator greatly and gave him profits to which the old regime had not accustomed him.

## 4. Wages

All organization of labor can be summarized into a single question: that of wages. The Socialists were well aware of that, so, as soon as they were in power, they hastened to promulgate a law that fixed the wages of the entire population and gave its poorest members the certainty of living honorably on the product of their work.

These were the principal provisions of that law:

All the employees of the Government—and they are very numerous in the Republic of the year 2000—are paid by the State with money brought in by taxes. Their wages vary between 2,400 francs and 12,000 francs per year. Some have fixed wages, which they collect on a monthly basis. Others, especially the workers, are paid by the day at a rate varying between eight and forty francs, and receive what is due to then every ten days. Finally, when practicable, work is paid on a piecework basis according to tariffs calculated on the basis that a day's earnings cannot be more than forty francs or less than eight.

Naturally, workers are paid more highly if they are more highly skilled in their profession, do their work more carefully or complete more tasks in a given time. It is precisely to make that estimation of individual merit easier that it is always preferable to pay piecework rates, and reward people according to what they have done, rather than the time they spent doing it. In any case, every time there is the slightest dispute over the tariffs applicable to some kind of work, the Government submits the question to a committee composed of workers in that trade, and complies fully with their decision, which is always in conformity with justice and properly motivated.

The workers and the employees of the State are submissive to foremen, managers, department heads and directors, who are paid more as they have a more numerous personnel under their orders, but without their wages ever surpassing the maximum figure of twelve thousand francs.

It is the Government that appoints employees responsible for giving instructions to others, and it is eager to choose, not only the most skilful workers, but those who also know how to make their comrades obey them and to be held in high esteem by them. As those sorts of individuals are uncommon, however, and there are not enough of the to fill all the places between foreman and department head, a good number of those employments are made on the basis of seniority—which is to say, to individuals whose sole merit is being older than others and having had more experience.

Age, in fact, inspires a certain respect in itself, and simultaneously earns indulgence and makes commands seem less harsh. So, the senior personnel appointed on seniority are generally well-liked, although they are quietly deemed to be "blockheads" and no one conforms very scrupulously to their orders.

In all the State shops, members of the sales staff are paid in a particular fashion appropriate to their profession. They do not receive fixed wages but earn a percentage of what they sell, so that they have a direct interest in maximizing the outflow of the merchandise placed in their hands. Those employees who do not make sales and are unable to earn a sufficient wage are invited to quit a career for which they are unsuited and look for another trade. As for very skillful salespersons, who succeed in making commissions in excess of twelve thousand francs, the income tax functions in their respect as for everyone else, and sets an insurmountable limit on what they can obtain.

Commercial employees also have managers, department heads and directors appointed by the government, but here the choice is easy and there is a reliable yardstick for measuring the merit of candidates. That guide is the level of their wages itself, a faithful expression of the talent they show in sales. All the functionaries directing the State shops are inevitably, therefore, very active, highly intelligent and very knowledgeable about business, and the important positions they occupy can be entrusted to them without fear.

It is those directors of commercial establishments who order, either from private industry or State factories, all the merchandise destined for consumption. Now, if these orders were placed by incompetent individuals and if, instead of being sold, they remained in stock and had to be disposed of at a discounted price, the Administration would incur considerable losses. Undoubtedly, the unintelligent director who was guilty of such a fault would not repeat it, for he would be immediately ruined, but thanks to the manner in which the directors of commercial organizations are selected, those sorts of miscalculations are impossible, and if some items ordered do not sell well and make a loss, it is amply counterbalanced by the profits made on all the other articles.

## 5. Wages (Continued)

The wages of established laborers working for themselves are not fixed by any regulation and only depend on their activity and intelligence. The Government furnishes them with raw materials at the lowest possible price, even on credit if they cannot pay cash, and then gladly buys the products of their manufacture from them at an agreed price.

Every season, manufacturers send their specimens and their current prices to the directors of retail establishments, and the later place their orders with the manufacturers who offer them the best terms. Naturally, talented workers, who work with good taste or are able to create a specialty, have no fear of being short of work and, far from having to chase after orders from directors, are sought out by them and made advantageous offers. These privileged artisans are perfectly free to put any price on their work they please, but they are subject like everyone else to the income tax, and their skill can never procure them an annual income in excess if twelve thousand francs.

When, instead of remaining isolated, workers find it worthwhile to come together in associations, the Government deals with them in exactly the same fashion. It furnished the with raw materials at a low price, gives them credit if they can offer sufficient guarantees of solvency, gives them orders and buys their products—but on the essential condition that the profits of all workers' associations must be divided between the members of the association in proportion to the time worked, without taking any account of the greater or less skill of the workers. In any case, in all those associations, it is the participating members who administer themselves, appointing their director and distributing work between them as agreed. The Administration only interests itself in one thing, which is that orders must be well-executed and the price paid for goods should be divided proportionally to the hours worked by each member.

Instead of forming associations or working for themselves, many workers in the year 2000 prefer to work for an employer who pays them an agreed wage every day. There are thus more tranquil, more exempt from worry; when they have done their day's work they are sure that they will be paid a fixed price, while independent workers or those in associations always have the bother of obtaining tools, buying raw materials, obtaining orders, etc., and often going to a great deal of trouble to earn as much, or even less, than if they were on wages.

The Socialist Government does not hinder in any way those workers who want to work for employers, and it respects their freedom of choice, as it respects that of workers who prefer to form associations or work independently. However, feeling responsible for the welfare of all citizens, the Authority has taken effective measures in order that wage-earners should not be exploited by their employers and should always receive a remuneration adequate to their needs. That result has been obtained by minimum salary tariffs to which employers are compelled to submit, and are obliged to pay without having permission to modify them.

Thus if the wage-earner is employed for a year, he must receive a wage of at least 2,400 francs. If he works by the day, that can only be for between eight and nine hours, and he must be paid at least eight francs. Finally, if the artisan works on a piecework basis, the price of his products must be calculated in a manner that will produce at least eight francs for an ordinary day's work.

These minimum tariffs apply to all professions, without exception; they apply to male and female workers alike, to workers in the fields as well as to those in cities. In establishing them, the Government intended that poverty should never afflict a working individual and that no one could ever pay employees at a lower rate, on any pretext whatsoever. When entrepreneurs complain that the tariffs are exorbitant and do not leave them any profit, the Administration replies that no one is obliged to be a employer, and that if they find the minimum wages so advantageous, they have only to become mere workers again and go to work like everyone else. Needless to say, none of them have taken advantage of that liberty, and, by dint of activity and intelligence, they have continued to do good business while paying their workers according to the regulation tariffs.

The minimum wages are, of course, merely a protective measure intended to ensure that workers' needs are met, but when workers are skillful and able to obtain higher daily rates, they are perfectly free to do so, and, as noted, can received up to forty francs a day.

As for an employer's profits, there is no limit to them; once his workers have been paid, everything he earns belongs to him, except that he is subject, like everyone else, to income tax, and his annual income cannot exceed the sum of twelve thousand francs.

Of all the socialist reforms that modified the old society from top to bottom in a matter of weeks, that limitation of the income of manufacturers was perhaps the one that raised the greatest number of protests against the Government. No manufacturer could understand why people wanted to restrict his profits and take away his liberty to enrich himself by enriching others.

When it was a matter of remunerating the services of the foremost State employees—an intelligent and experienced administrator, an eminent judge, a skilled engineer, a remarkable scientist, etc.—oh, then our manufacturers could find good reasons for putting a limit on those functionaries' salaries and never giving them more than twelve thousand francs. Many even claimed that it was too much, and declared that they were opposed to high wages that were ruining the public Treasury—but when it was a question of the income of a lemonade manufacturer, a candle-maker, a wine-producer or any other industrialist, our malcontents would no longer put any limits on their generosity. Thirty, fifty, a hundred, two hundred thousand francs in annual profits did not seem to them to be too much adequately to reward the exceptional talents of a manufacturer, and to restrict his fortune, to render him equal to the foremost State functionaries, was to commit the most revolting iniquity and to be guilty of a crime against civilization.

The Government took absolutely no notice of these recriminations, and, as it had public opinion in its favor, it watched more carefully than ever over the strict imposition of the income tax. Rendered furious by that measure, which ate into their profits, certain large manufacturers threatened to leave the country and take their industry to England or America, but on more mature reflection, they found that such repatriation would be very risky and judged it more prudent to stay in France and to live modestly on the income of twelve thousand francs that the Socialist Republic consented to leave them.

## 6. General Insurance

The Government of the Social Republic did not limit itself to ensuring good wages to workers who worked, but it came to their aid when they were out of work and gave them the means to put a end to their unemployment.

Unemployment, so frequent in the old industrial regime, was due to the fact that work was badly organized and that speculation created exaggerated demands, surpassing the current needs of consumption. Instead of distributing manufacture over the whole year, employers overworked the laborers during good times, making them work twelve- and fifteen-hour days, and then, once the orders were filled, they sent them away and left them without bread.

In the Republic of the Year 2000 that sort of unemployment is never produced, because it is the Government that controls commerce and places orders, which are always regulated and calculated in such a way as to occupy manufacturers all the year round. There are, however, some causes of unemployment that nothing can prevent, such as, for example, bad harvests, commercial crises in other countries, changes in fashion, the invention of new machines, etc. In all these circumstances, the Administration immediately comes to the assistance of the workers thrown out of work, and thus gives them time to await the resumption of business or to find work in some other branch of industry.

At other times, artisans are forced to interrupt their work in consequence of illness, precocious infirmities or injuries contracted in the exercise of their profession. In that case, the State hastens once again to come to their aid. It allocates them assistance throughout the duration of their illness, or a pension for the rest of their life if they remain infirm and cannot resume their occupation.

Finally, when workers grow old and reach the age of sixty or sixty-five years of age, they retire, and once again receive a pension that permits them to end their days in idleness.

These various kinds of help are accorded to all French people without exception, to independent workers as well as to Government employees. The aid is proportionate to the income of the individual aided, and as that income pays a proportional income tax, it is not charity, but a restitution by the State, which returns to the invalid, the infirm or aged individual the sums it has received from the young and healthy citizen. Undoubtedly, unhealthy individuals or those struck by precocious infirmities take a larger share from the produce of that tax than others do, but that is a sad privilege, which is scarcely enviable, for it is bought too early by the loss of health or premature death.

At any rate, all the assistance allocated to individuals incapable of working is quite sufficient, and it does not require the Nation to increase it further by increasing the income tax. Thus, to cite only one example, every sick worker receives enough to be treated at home by a physician of his choice, and never needs to go to a hospice, as was necessary under the old regime. It has therefore been possible to abolish those sad hospitals, which established an injurious distinction between the rich and the poor, and delivered the latter to the experiments of physicians and the inexperience of students carrying out their medical education on the vile multitude, scalpel-fodder sacrificed to the health of the wealthier classes.

Even hospices for the old, to which old men had so much difficulty being admitted, and in which they led a miserable life, far from their friends and children, have been abolished. In the Social Republic, similar turpitudes are not tolerated, and rather than permit their reestablishment, the people who constitute the Authority would rather increase the income tax and reduce the maximum of individual fortunes to ten thousand francs, or even eight thousand.

In any case while remaining in the milieu of Society, retired people are not entirely useless there. They continue to go to workshops and shops, where they carry out a few small tasks and give advice to the younger people. Many of them have extremely undemanding jobs, like wardens of gallery-streets, curators or demonstrators of public collections, providers of information in offices, etc. In this well-organized Society everyone can find a useful occupation proportionate to his intelligence and strength, and, except for dangerous lunatics and the dying, there is no one who cannot occupy his time and employ his faculties.

Certain accidents—such as fires, floods, hail, crop failures, livestock diseases, etc.—may strike, not the citizens themselves, but the property they possess. The Government aids the victims of these disasters and gives them the means to repair the misfortune that has unjustly overtaken them. Thanks to this State assistance, the old Insurance Companies have become unnecessary, so they have been suppressed, the shareholders being reimbursed with annual incomes, limited, as ever, to a maximum of twelve thousand francs.

The majority of the Parisians of the year 2000 are exceedingly extravagant. Far from thinking about putting aside any savings, they spend their wages and reimbursements in advance, living half the time on credit owed to their suppliers and never having a sou in their pocket. A few citizens are exceptional, however, and only spend a part of their income.

Some, industrious and intelligent, employ their savings in purchasing raw materials and tools; they set up in business, or, if they are already established, they increase the scope of their business and thus increase the level of their annual income.

Others, less ambitious or more timid, prefer to keep their money and confide it to the State, which coverts it into annual payments, which can be constituted, either to the entitlement of the depositor of the funds or to any other person—a child, a wife, a friend, etc. They can even, if desired, be transferable, and for example, credited to a mother and then, if she dies, to her children. These kinds of payments are an extremely convenient and sure way of placing money, for the Government cannot fail to keep its promises as individuals might do, and it is always ready to liquidate capital deposited with it.

Let us make this observation: the lifelong incomes of the Social Republic are essentially different from the perpetual incomes created by the old regimes. The latter provided an interest every year without the capital being diminished, and indefinitely, so that the recipients and their children always remained rich without having any need to work, living in idleness and the vices that it engenders. The result was a class of *rentiers*, who believed themselves to be the most important and most estimable people in the land, because they had the means to live without doing anything.

The Socialists put an end to that intolerable disorder. They suppressed perpetual incomes and transformed them into lifelong incomes, submissive, as is only just, to income tax—a financial operation that the Government always exercises with pleasure, because it has the double advantage of enriching the State and impoverishing useless and insolent idlers.

# III. SOCIETY

## 1. Social Relations

What characterizes the Social Republic and renders it a Government unique in the world, is that all the citizens work and have incomes that are almost equal, the richest among them having no more than twelve thousand francs per year while the poorest earn at least 2,400. The ratio of the largest and smallest incomes is thus 5:1.

Now, that difference is not sufficiently considerable to permit the rich to live a life apart and form a so-called upper class that proudly entitles itself "Society," while the multitude of the poor are scorned, counting for nothing in the State and having but one lot: to work, always to work, in order to maintain the luxury and idleness of the dominant caste.

Thanks to the income tax and the suppression of all rents, that division of Society into classes has completely disappeared and, although the Republicans of the year 2000 are not completely equal in rank and wealth, they all feel a solidarity with one another, and no one has any reluctance to associate with people richer or poorer than himself.

Moreover, what contributes a great deal to creating union and concord between the citizens is the education they receive. As will be seen in the following chapter, all children, whatever the social situation of their parents, are educated in public schools where they lead exactly the same life, following the same lessons, subject to the same examinations, and are subject to the most complete equality.

Later, they all enter schools of apprenticeship, and then become simple workers or employees; no one can attain more wealth or a superior placement without having passed through petty employments, and making friends and acquaintances therein. Once having succeeded, they continue to live on familiar terms with their initial comrades, and the difference in wealth is never considerable enough to sever old relationships created by mutual sympathy.

In the choice of people with whom one keeps company, therefore, one does not consider either rank or income, but simply the friendship one has for them and the pleasure experienced in seeing one another.

Although, in such a society, some people are a little richer and others a little poorer, no one suffers from that difference because no one makes it felt, the opulence of the most fortunate never being great enough to excite the jealousy or covetousness of others.

When the Social Republic was first established, a certain number of individuals who called themselves "nobles" and bore a "de" in front of their surname refused to submit to that life of equality, however comfortable and agreeable it might be. Their rents might have been taken away and they might have been given petty employments in relation to their abilities, but they continued to band together, only associating with one another and having the most profound scorn for the rest of humankind.

As all these titled people were irreconcilable enemies of the new institutions, the Government did not have to treat them kindly, and this is what it did to confound their pride and suppress those distinctions of nobility of which they were so fond.

To begin with, their parchments—the charters and citations that they valued more than life itself—were taken away, and all those wads of paper were pitilessly burned in front of them. But that was not all; wanting to punish them in a fashion appropriate to their sin, the vanity of their name, the Government debaptized them and made them adopt new names that were chosen expressly from among the most vulgar and ridiculous.

The fury and resentment of that proud Nobility, when they were allotted names so little adapted to pride, is indescribable. It was an intolerable torture, continually renewed, and some left the country rather than submit to it. Others—those with more intelligence—were cleverer. They were the first to laugh at their new names and got used to bearing them, telling jokers that, if their names lent themselves to ridicule, it was not their fault, but that of the Republic.

In the new Society that the Socialists have created, everyone works, without exception, and is proud to work. People no longer having rents of any kind, nor any means of living honorably in idleness, are all compelled to find employment.

With regard to women, the Government strives to give them all professions in relation to their aptitudes. Some, in very large numbers, exercise various industries such as those of dressmaker, florist, engraver, embroiderer, box-maker, jeweler, etc. Others, almost as numerous are employed in retail establishments or work in the factories of heavy industry. Others are teachers in public schools. Finally, others are employed by the Administration as stewards, accountants, inspectors, directors, etc., and can only be praised for the manner in which they fulfill their functions.

## 2. Property

Property is the basis of the entire economic order of the Social Republic and every citizen has "the right to enjoy it and dispose of it in the most absolute possible fashion, provided that he does not make any use of it prohibited by the laws or regulations."[7]

If the Government has multiplied these laws and regulations, it is solely in order that everyone can conserve the fruits of his labor in their entirety and is not exposed to being deprived of them by any means.

The citizens of the year 2000 can therefore possess all kinds of property in total security: land, houses, livestock, utensils of labor, merchandise, furniture, clothing, etc., etc. Similarly, they can exchange all these objects between them, for money or for other goods.

However, although the exchange of property could not be more legitimate, it is not the same with speculation and commerce, which are strictly forbidden to individuals and reserved to the State.

That distinction between commerce and exchange is easy to establish. The latter is a transient, accidental matter that can easily lead to a loss as a profit. Commerce, on the other hand, is a habit, a profession one follows: a profession in which everything in planned and organized to bring in a profit. As it can only be fruitful insofar as it takes place on a certain scale, and acquires a certain publicity, it is immediately distinguishable from simple bar-

---

[7] The author inserts a footnote: "The definition of property given by the Civil Code."

ter, and it is the very notoriety of the delinquent that denounces him and attracts the severity of Justice upon him.

The sales and exchanges that citizens make between themselves must always be made in cash. All promissory notes of payment are considered null and have no value in court; a person who has not been paid on surrendering an item is regarded as having made a gift of it. That suppression of sale on credit does not impede serious and honest bargains in any way, for the National Bank lends money to all those in need of it, always provided, of course, that they can provide moral or material guarantees of reimbursement. But the abolition of credit between individuals—and this is the reason for it—has cut off speculation, usury, shady dealing and all the dishonest transactions that, under the old regime, deprived workers to the profit of people who did not work.

For the same reasons, it is absolutely forbidden to let out any immovable property. A person who possesses a house or a piece of land must live in it or cultivate it personally, or get rid of it and sell it to whoever wants to buy it.

When, in spite of that prohibition, a citizen lets out his property, the lease is void in legal terms and the occupant remains the possessor of the leased item, being deemed to have received it as a straightforward gift. Thanks to that radical measure, the renting of land has completely disappeared in rural areas, and agriculture has only become more prosperous, since there are no longer any idle landlords who have their land farmed instead of cultivating it themselves, growing fat at their leisure on the sweat of peasants.

On the death of parents, legitimate or legitimated children inherit all their property by right, and it is divided equally between them. The father and mother can, however, dispose of a portion of their fortune fixed by law and let it pass by testament to one of their children, relatives or strangers.

In order to avoid all the lawsuits caused by badly-drafted testaments, the latter must be made in accordance with invariable forms, which the Government delivers to individuals ready-printed. To make one's testament, one has only to obtain one of these forms, fill in the blanks, date and sign it, and then return it to the civil estate; one is then certain that lawyers cannot consume all or part of the estate in fees.

When a spouse dies intestate, their wealth is divided between the children and the surviving spouse, the latter being treated on an equal basis with the children. If the deceased was a bachelor or spinster without children, it is the relatives who inherit, and, in the absence of those, the State.

As soon as children have reached the age of majority at eighteen, they can sell what they possess in their own right and dispose of it by testament or donation without their parents raising any impediment. That right is exactly the same for the two sexes, and a woman, whether she is married or not, has the free disposition of all her property without her family, her husband or her children having any say in the matter.

Thanks to these rights of young women and wives, marriage contracts have become extremely simple. Everyone is married under the regime of the community. Each spouse possesses his or her own property and administers at will the property acquired by dowry or by inheritance. As for property acquired during the marriage, it remains undivided between the spouses and either of them can dispose of it without the formal consent of the other. In case of separation, communal property follows the children, and, in consequence, remains with the mother, as will be seen in part 6 of this chapter; if there are no children, it is divided equally between the couple.

### 3. Money

In the Republic of the year 2000, there is no gold or silver money; the only money that is used for all transactions is paper money consisting of banknotes issued by the National Bank.

The latter represent sums of 1, 2, 5, 10, 20 and 50 centimes and 1, 2, 5, 10, 20, 50 and 100 francs. They are of different sizes and colors according to their value, with the result that it is impossible to confuse them and to make mistakes in exchange. All these banknotes are made with reinforced paper resistant to wear. In any case, when they are torn, soiled or faded, the Government unhesitatingly exchanges them for new ones.

When the Social Republic was established, many people made dire predictions about these banknotes, and thought that they would not take long to fail, as all systems of paper money had so far done—but the Government, buying and selling everything from and to individuals, and holding the country's commerce entirely in its own hands, was perfectly certain of success this time. It ordered its employees not to accept gold and silver coins any longer, and those, in order to be utilized, had to be exchanged for notes. After a certain time, the Administration refused to make that exchange at par, and only treated metallic money henceforth as merchandise—which is to say, subjecting it to a small loss on its nominal value.

Thanks to these measures, it did not take long for all the gold and silver in France to flow into the Treasury's coffers. The Government did not leave them there, but sold them at a reasonable price to gilders, goldsmiths, jewelers, etc.—which provided a vigorous stimulus to those various industries and led to a considerable lowering of the price of all jewelry and other objects manufactured with precious metals.

Often, instead of keeping their banknotes in their pockets or a drawer, individuals prefer to deposit them at the nearest branch of the National Bank and pay for their various acquisitions with the aid of bearer checks. Thus, an employer can pay his workers' wages, not in cash, but in drafts that they can negotiate at a nearby Bank branch. Instead of taking the trouble to go to collect his pay, the worker is also able to leave it in a current account and pay his suppliers with checks. That method of payment is very handy, especially for small sums, since it is authenticated and dispenses with the need to ask for a receipt.

As for the business that manufacturers transact with the Government, it is regulated in a simpler manner, not with banknotes or checks but with the aid of transfers. Each manufacturer has his current account at one of the branches of the National Bank; the sums due to him or to be collected from him are inscribed there, and he can draw on the difference.

Thanks to these current accounts, the exact financial situation of every manufacturer is always known. As soon as one of them gets into difficulties, the Bank ceases to extend them credit, and thus avoids all the disastrous bankruptcies that desolated the commerce of the old regime, suddenly ruining perfectly honest people.

These payments with the aid of checks and transfers seem very complicated when one explains them in writing, but in practice they are as expeditious as they are convenient, and a few branches of the National Bank, distributed in the various quarters of the city, are easily sufficient for all the needs of commerce, and regulate an immense number of transactions on a daily basis without there ever being the slightest loss to vendors or purchasers.

## 4. Dwellings

In rural areas, every cultivator has his own house, and when a new citizen comes to take up residence in a locality, the National Bank willingly lends him money to buy a dwelling, or to construct one if there are none vacant.

In cities, hardly anyone owns his lodgings; it is the State that owns all the houses and rents them to individuals.

These houses are divided into independent rooms, but all of them can communicate with one another by means of interior doors, and, in accordance with one's desire to have a larger or smaller apartment, one rents as many contiguous rooms as one needs.

The cost of rents is always very moderate, especially in the outlying quarters, and one can obtain comfortable lodgings for fifty or sixty francs a year. In the city center and the busiest streets, it is true, the rents are considerably higher because of competition between the inhabitants, and also because the houses are much more sumptuous and the rooms more richly decorated.

Furthermore, the Government does not employ any strategy to increase the returns of its rents. It never in-

creases its rents as a matter of policy or threatens to ex-
pel those who refuse to pay more dearly. When a dwelling becomes vacant, the employees of the City put it out
for rent by means of a kind of auction, awarding it to the
highest bidder, and once installed, the latter remains
tranquilly in possession of his new domicile so long as
he does not decide to move of his own accord.

As the Administration is constantly constructing
model houses, and puts new apartments at the disposal
of the public on a daily basis, competition between Parisians is not very intense; save for the plushest quarters,
the cost of accommodation remain low. In spite of these
low returns, however, the construction of model houses
is so economical that the State not only covers its expenses but makes a considerable profit every year, which
constitutes an important resource for the Treasury.

Apart from paying the rent, the City does not impose any obligation or regulation on its tenants. Provided
that the latter do not damage the building or inconvenience their neighbors, they can do as they wish, go in
any out at any hour of the night, receive whatever visitors they please, and have children or pets. The manager
of a house is never the first to complain about anything
whatsoever, and if an observation sometimes has to be
made to a tenant it is always at the request of the other
inhabitants.

Thanks to the entire liberty granted to citizens,
nothing is more varied and mixed than the population of
model houses. All conditions, all professions, all fortunes, all ranks and all ways of life are thrown together
pell-mell, next door to one another, living in peace under
the shelter of the same roof. Unless you harm your
neighbors, no one has any observation to make on your
account. There are not, as there once were, several cate-

gories of habitations in which the different classes of society resided: large town houses, rich houses, nice houses and utterly wretched houses. Everywhere, there are only Government-owned houses inhabited by citizens, all of whom exercise some profession or other and all of whom are subject to the sacred equality of work.

Remarkably, the result of that absolute liberty has been to group inhabitants quite naturally according to their way of life. Thus, without anything being done to obtain that end, there are streets that are only occupied by tranquil married people, in which everyone is in bed by nine o'clock. Other houses, on the other hand, are devoted to the unmarried, to pleasure and noise, where entire nights are often spent singing and drinking, without the neighbors making the slightest complaint because they are all guilty of the same faults in their turn.

It is rare for Parisians to exercise their profession in the same building in which they live, even if they are self-employed, preferring to go to a workshop, where they are always more comfortable accommodated and can work alongside others, which is always pleasanter and more economical. Many of them also do not cook and eat at home, and their rooms, solely employed for sleeping and serving as a retreat, are not only furnished very comfortably but even with a veritable luxury.

Nothing is more commonplace that seeing simple workers inhabiting apartments furnished with silk or velvet wall-hangings, paintings and works of art. Thanks to the prodigious development of industry, all that beautiful furniture is relatively cheap, and is easy to procure with the aid of a little thrift.

The Republican women of the year 2000 are enormously devoted to that interior luxury. After clothing, it is their favorite expense, and, as they are generally the ones in charge of their husbands' purse, and who organize the expenditure of the household, it is rare for them not to achieve their objectives and not to be able to lodge and dress themselves like princesses.

## 5. Domestic Service

Among the Socialists of the year 2000 there are no domestic servants. No one, however highly-placed he might be, has the right to hire another citizen, to take him into his service, to give him orders and be his master. Considering domesticity as a last vestige of slavery and a grave attack on Equality, the Government abolished it explicitly by means of a memorable decree in the first days of its advent.

It must not be thought, however, that the citizens of the Social Republic do all their own housework. On the contrary; few things are more disagreeable to them, and even the poorest accord themselves the luxury of other people's services. That service is, however, carried out by free employees and not by domestic servants, which is quite different. Indeed, those employees do not belong to anyone in particular; they take responsibility for household chores as they would accomplish any other social function, and although they serve everyone, they are, in reality, their own masters.

Thus, a certain number of people are professional bed-makers, room-cleaners, floor-polishers, chamber-pot-emptiers, furniture polishers, shoe-waxers, clothing-cleaners, etc. As soon as inhabitants have left for work, these employees come into the rooms confided to their cares and, thanks to their number and the manner in which they divide up the work, an apartment is done in

importance, the Government desires that the interested parties should make their own decision, and that they should not be subjected to any pressure or constraint, even exercised with the best of intentions.

In general, young men do not marry until much later, between the ages of thirty and forty, when they have acquired a position in accord with their abilities, they have experience of life, and, turning away from the pleasures and follies of youth, they ask no more than to settle down and find the tranquil happiness of the conjugal hearth in the intimacy of an affectionate wife.

Young women, by contrast, marry as soon as they can, often the day after reaching their majority. If they reach the age of twenty-five without having found a husband, they are desolate and think themselves condemned to perpetual spinsterhood. When they reach thirty, however, they lose their heads completely, wishing to marry at any price, and throw themselves into the arms of any man who comes along. However, it' is very rare for young women to arrive at that extremity, and they are usually established in good time, between the ages of eighteen and twenty.

Socialists of both sexes marry very hastily, often at first sight, without studying one another or getting to know one another, and, in consequence, without knowing whether they have a sincere sympathy for one another.

Men only ask of their future wife that she be young and pretty, well-dressed, and will do honor to the cavalier who gives her is arm. Young women, for their part, want their husband to be well turned-out and to occupy a certain rank in society. At that price, they forgive him for being a trifle mature, a trifle weary, for having a few white hairs, and even for balding slightly.

When the French of the year 2000 are reproached for the truly incredible insouciance with which they marry, they reply that it is an imperious necessity of marriage, and that if one had to be thoroughly acquainted with the person whom they were to marry, no one would any longer want to, and everyone would remain unmarried.

Naturally, unions contracted so lightly can neither be very happy nor very durable. Thus, it very often happens that the spouses cannot live with one another and demanded their separation. That is obtained with the greatest ease. It is sufficient for one of the couple to write a letter to a magistrate, in which they request a separation on the grounds of temperamental incompatibility, and the marriage is immediately dissolved, even if the other spouse is opposed to it and wants to remain united.

The Socialist Government has even been obliging enough to make available pre-printed requests for separation, on which it is only necessary to fill in the names, the date and a signature. One then puts it in the post, and without further need for disturbance, one receives the desired authorization in the following day's mail. Furthermore, quite often, no sooner have the spouses been separated for a few days than they resume living together, and then constitute an excellent household that only death can sever.

The Government has been asked to reestablish divorce on many occasions, but it has consistently refused. In its considered opinion, there is no point in people who treat marriage so lightly remarrying, and if the levity of the French character does not permit them to render conjugal bonds indissoluble, that is all the more reason for not making such bonds the banal accompaniment of fleeting relationships and legitimating the deregulation of mores by giving it the approval of the Republic's magistrates.

On the other hand, in every separated household, one spouse at least, if not both, is absolutely unsociable and will always be the other's torturer. Now, to divorce these torturers, to permit them to marry again and to torture further victims, would be to unleash on the nation the worst of scourges and to work determinedly to create misfortune.

In any case, the separated individuals, although not being able to remarry, have no reason to complain. Society treats them with the greatest indulgence and closes its eyes to their conduct. In fact, they are considered as perfectly free widowers and widows, and if they subsequently take up residence with someone, everyone treats them as if they were legitimately married.

In the Republic of the year 2000, children born during a marriage belong to the mother alone, who gives them her name and sees to their needs. The husband, however, if he so desires can obtain permission to adopt his wife's children, to give them his name and consider them as his own. That is what always happens in practice—but the adoption by the father of the family is entirely honorific; it does not give him any real rights over his wife's children. She always remains the mistress of her progeny, and invariably takes them with her in case of separation.

This consecration of the rights of the mother to the detriment of those of the father was not established without violent protests on the part of husbands, who complained about having the guardianship of their children removed from them. The Government simply replied to them that they had to furnish authentic proof of the paternity whose rights they were claiming, and, as that proof was impossible to provide, they were obliged to content themselves with the honorary guardianship that was offered to them.

In Socialist society, mothers only occupy themselves with their children to embrace them, dress them, take them for walks, lavish treats upon them and spoil them horribly by giving in to all their caprices. Fathers act in exactly the same way, and are, if possible, even weaker and more easy-going. As for educating children, directing their studies or the choice of a profession, neither the father nor the mother gives any thought to that, and that concern is entirely left to the teachers and directors of the establishments of public education.

In the Republic of the year 2000, prostitution does not exist, every woman finding a lucrative occupation if she can work and assistance if she is incapable of earning a living. If, however, in Socialist society one cannot encounter a single prostitute, strictly speaking, one does, on the other hand see numerous so called "loose women," who are possessed or neither virtue nor constancy, and who are as easy to seduce as they are hard to maintain in fidelity.

Women of that sort seem to have taken on the task of competing in immortality and knavery with the men who court them, and one must do them the justice of admitting that, in that kind of contest, their superiority is striking. After a certain time, however, they get tired of that disorderly life; they then apply themselves to living with their latest lover, to whom they are quite faithful, and when those irregular unions have lasted for a number of years, society, full of indulgence, forgets the past of such unfortunate women and treats them as if they had always kept narrowly to the path of virtue.

# IV. EDUCATION

## 1. Early Infancy

In the Republic of the year 2000, bringing up and educating children is confided to the responsibility of the State and is completely free. The Socialist Republic operates on the principle that children are perfectly free and independent individuals whose guardianship is the responsibility of Society, and over whom the parents have only one right, which is that of loving them.

The education provided is essentially free and involves no cost to the parents. It is paid for by the children themselves—not directly, of course, but indirectly, with the intermediary of the Administration, which advances the funds necessary and is reimbursed later by their work of adults. When fathers and bachelors pay taxes destined for public education, they are not giving anything for their own children or those of others, but are paying for their own education, and merely making restitution to the State of what has previously been spent on them. As the tax is proportional to income, income to ability, and ability to education, everyone pays more if they are drawing greater profited from the lessons they have received, and no one has any right to complain.

The Parisians of the year 2000 are not very fecund. They only have one child, or two at the most, and also become very ill in bringing them to term and delivering them. Among them, the civilized woman has killed the nurse. The majority lack milk and the others, apparently more favored, perish along with their nurslings when they attempt to breast-feed them.

For a long time, Parisian women, who love their children to the point of adoration and want to bring them up at any cost, gave their babies to country-dwelling wet-nurses, but, either because the latter were as etiolated as the inhabitants of the capital, or because they did not take god enough care of the delicate nurslings confided to their care, they returned very few of them, and all the little Parisians went to populate the cemeteries of the provinces.

That went on for a long time, and the women of Paris were despairing of being able to conserve their children when the Government came to their aid. It knew that in Normandy mothers rarely breast-feed, but almost all their bottle-fed babies drink the milk of their cows, which is excellent. Far from perishing on that regime, young Normans are all the more vigorous for it, and form the magnificent race that everyone knows.

The Administration thought that what succeeded elsewhere would not fail in Paris. In consequence, it brought the finest Norman cows to the villages surrounding the capital, along with women from the same region accustomed to bottle-feeding. Both were accommodated comfortably and healthily, and Parisian mothers were then invited to bring their babies to them. That first trial having been a great success, the number of "nurseries" around the city was increased, and Parisian women had the double joy of having all their infants removed and seeing them grow, so to speak, before their eyes.

When young Parisians have renounced the feeding-bottle, can walk by themselves and have begun to talk, the mothers bring them back to the city, but as the mothers all have jobs and work outside the home, it is impossible for them to keep their children with them during the day, so they confide them to "governesses."

The latter have nothing in common with the governesses of the old regime, poor decrepit old women only earning a few sous for watching over miserable runts. They are, on the contrary, active and intelligent young women carefully chosen and well paid by the Administration, and they fulfill the important functions confided to them with an entirely maternal solicitude. Mothers themselves—for in crèches, as in schools, no employment is given to unmarried women—and fond of caring for small children, they watch over other people's babies as assiduously as if were their own.

The governesses of the year 2000 are capaciously accommodated and provided with the environment necessary to their functions. Depending on the weather, they keep the children indoors or take them to play in the gardens of the model houses, never leaving the young clients placed under their surveillance for an instant. Subject to a firm and affectionate authority, and also obliged to live in society with their little comrades and to give up on many caprices, infants are no longer, as before, either completely neglected and unworthily mistreated, or, on the contrary, excessively spoiled, whiny and willful. They thus receive a solid early education—something so important for the rest of life, and which their parents, often coarse, brutal or overly weak-willed, would be absolutely incapable of giving them.

However, family ties are not broken by the existence of these crèches. Whenever fathers or mothers leave work temporarily, they come to the governess to ask after their children and spend some time with them. In the evening, when their day's work is done, they take them home until the following day, chatting and eating with them and putting them to bed in a crib next to the mother's bed. Only seeing their parents in that interval, and in moments of good humor, children love them all the more, and, if they have resentments against anyone, it is more likely to be the governess, who is sometimes obliged to be stern and chastise the little rascals confided to her care.

## 2. Primary Schools

Education is the Socialist Government's principal means of action; that is how it has taken definitive possession of the minds of populations and assured the ruination of the obsolete doctrines that ruled ancient Societies.

Under the Social Republic, education is free, secular and obligatory.

It is free in that it costs parents absolutely nothing, regardless of their financial situation and the number of their children.

It is secular in that it rests on essentially rational and scientific bases, and rejects all information given by religious corporations or individuals imbued with clerical notions.

It is obligatory in that the State, the guardian of all children, constrains them to attend schools and takes them there by force if unnatural parents do not send them of their own free will.

On these three fundamental points the Government has never tolerated the slightest argument, for education thus comprised is the very basis of the Republic and the sole guarantee of its endurance. If the law regarding public education were to be changed, the rebirth of the old regime, with all its abuses, would be seen within a matter of years. The Administration knows that and, being responsible for the fate of young generations, watches with jealous care over that precious deposit and simultaneously protects it from ignorance and doctrines hostile to the spirit of Socialism.

*Primary schools.*

As soon as children can speak fluently and begin to be able to understand, they are put into primary schools, where they learn to read and write.

These schools are extremely numerous. There are two of them, one for boys and the other for girls, in every country village and every city street. Large, hygienic, well-ventilated, well-heated in winter and provided with a courtyard and a garden, the children stay there all day and only leave in the evenings to return to their parental homes.

All the primary schools, for boys as well as or girls, are maintained not by male teachers, who are no good for small children, but by female ones. The latter, all mothers who have a vocation for education, fulfill their functions as much out of devotion as duty, and monitor the health and cleanliness of their pupils as carefully as their instruction. They are paid by the Government and chosen from among the most intelligent and highly-respected of the many women who seek this kind of employment. They form a powerful corporation in the State, by virtue of their number and influence, and, although their profession is no better remunerated than any other, they are the object of universal consideration, and occupy the forefront of society.

In general, classes are not very large and comprise no more than twenty or twenty-five children, so that the teacher can easily supervise and instruct all the pupils entrusted to her care. Furthermore, she can be assisted in that task by those pupils who are more advanced than their comrade and serve as monitors.

Every month, at indeterminate epochs, female inspectors come to visit the schools and make sure that they are well-maintained. At the same time, they interrogate the pupils carefully and take account of the progress they have made. These examinations are extremely important for the children. According to whether they come through them with more or less success, they either remain in the same class or pass into another, where they receive a more advanced education.

By courtesy of these examinations, all the pupils of a single school are divided into several classes, entitled reading, writing, grammar, calculation and so on, into which they are only admitted after having given proof of a certain knowledge. Now, the children make it a point of honor among themselves not to remain in the inferior classes, and, in order to escape that shame, they work with an ardor and assiduity was rarely seen in the schools of the old regime.

The teachers themselves take a strong interest in the monthly examinations and make every effort to render them more brilliant—for, according to whether their pupils are more or less advanced for their age and respond to their interrogators more or less competently, they will be marked up or down themselves by the Administration, and either left where they are or promoted. In the latter case they are entrusted with larger schools or appointed as instructors or directors.

The children remain in primary schools until they can read and write well, and know the elements of grammar, history, geography, calculation and natural history. At the end of the year, the most advanced are subjected to so-called exit-examinations on all these subjects, and if they do honor to themselves they are admitted into s secondary school. If not, they remain in the primary school until the age of their apprenticeship.

### 3. Secondary Schools

Secondary schools, less numerous than primary schools, are only found in cities and large towns, where the population is sufficiently concentrated to furnish the number of pupils necessary to the creation of an establishment.

These schools receive day pupils, half-boarders and full-boarders. As with everything concerned with education, they are entirely free and parents do not pay any more when their children are fed, accommodated and clothed by the State.

In secondary schools, of course, the sexes are rigorously separated. The establishments for boys are never close to those for girls, and great care is taken to ensure that there is no communication between them.

The schools for boys are maintained by schoolmasters, who are well paid and highly esteemed. To obtain their position they are obliged to submit to rigorous examinations, and the rank they occupy in the esteem of their fellow citizens is entirely in accord with their merit and the important functions they fulfill. As for the girls' schools, they are directed by female teachers, with the collaboration of a few males.

In general, the establishments for boys include a large number of boarders and very few day pupils, families asking for nothing better than to be completely rid of turbulent children who are difficult to restrain and, once at liberty, think of nothing but roaming far and wide or breaking everything in the house.

In the schools for girls, there are, by contrast, few boarders and a great many half-boarders, parents being much more comfortable spending the evenings with their daughters—who, being gentle and sedentary, do not like to distance themselves from their mothers.

At any rate, the boarders of both sexes are quite happy in the State establishments. They are well-nourished, hygienically accommodated, have courtyards in which to play, gardens in which to stroll, receive frequent visits from their parents and spend all their holidays with them.

The subjects taught in secondary schools are grammar, literature, calculation, history, geography, natural history, the gentle arts, music and drawing, living languages and the elementary notions of the exact sciences. These subjects are absolutely identical for boys and girls, and have freed the latter from the obligation they once had to learn sewing, knitting, tapestry and embroidery. Those kinds of needlework are no longer considered as the indispensable complement of a good female education, but simply as distractions, to which pupils only devote themselves if it pleases and amuses them.

Like pupils in primary schools, those in secondary schools are subject to monthly examinations and subdivided into classes that are more or less advanced. The children, who already have a great deal of self-respect at that age, make superhuman efforts not to be held back, thus earning the derision of their more advanced comrades, who do not hesitate to give them ridiculous nicknames. The teachers are just as keenly interested in the examinations, which are entitlements to advancement for them, and they leave no stone unturned to make their pupils work and to instruct them.

At the end of every year, the most learned pupils pass general examinations on all the subjects they have been taught. Only those who respond appropriately to these examinations are allowed o enter the higher schools. As for those who have obtained less profit from their masters' lessons, they remain in the secondary schools, where they conclude their education on reaching the age at which they have to choose a profession.

## 4. Higher Schools

Higher schools exactly resemble secondary ones, save that they receive older pupils, already more learned, and that more emphasis is put there on education in literature, natural and exact sciences, and the fine arts.

The pupils are subjected to the same monthly and annual examinations, which serve to classify the pupils, measuring their various aptitudes and directing their studies in consequence.

Thus, depending on whether the pupils show a greater disposition for the sciences, letters or fine arts, they are pushed in one of those three directions and permitted to devote more time to their favorite subjects. That method has the advantage of not wearying the pupils with unnecessary lessons, and simultaneously, ensuring them more rapid progress in the knowledge for which they have a vocation; the pupils then work with an extraordinary ardor, which their masters are obliged to moderate lest it damage their health.

After two or three years spent in higher schools, young people have finished their education, and, having reached the age to choose a profession, they embrace one or other of them, in accordance with the studies they had undertaken.

In sum, in the Social Republic, the general system of public education is composed of progressive classes and schools into which the children can only be admitted after being subjected to examinations of increasing difficulty. The studious and intelligent pupil, who always responds well in all his examinations, can therefore take all his classes and reach the higher schools.

Children less well-endowed or less laborious only take classes that are to some extent incomplete. They remain in the secondary schools, or even in the primary schools, and when they reach the age to choose a trade they obtain one in harmony with the level of education they have attained.

Undoubtedly, the result of this is a great inequality between citizens, some of whom are fairly ignorant and devoted to the manual arts, whereas others, fully educated, exercise liberal professions. The fault lies, however, entirely with the children, who are unable or unwilling to profit from the lessons lavished upon them, and no one has any right to complain, because everyone has been given the same opportunity to obtained a complete education.

That is the exact opposite of what happened under the old regime; in those times, the children of poor people were obliged to leave school for the workshop and it was necessary for them to remain ignorant even if they had the most marvelous disposition for study, while the sons of good families spent their entire youth in colleges where they learned absolutely nothing and only studied ways to enrage the honorable professors charged with instructing all those little idlers.

## 5. *Apprenticeship*

In the Social Republic, because everyone has to work and to have a profession, all young people, on leaving school, enter into apprenticeship.

That apprenticeship is undertaken under the direction of the State and in establishments belonging to it. To that effect, in all industries, even the most trivial, the Government has created so-called "model workshops," which hire the best workers within the specialty, which are provided with improved machinery and in which all new methods of fabrication are tested.

These model workshops are not indeed to compete with private industry; their sole objective is to favor the progress of each trade and, above all, to take apprentices. Thus, model bakeries have been created, along with model farms, model dressmaking studios, etc., in sufficient numbers to receive all those destined for various employments. There, workers who are as benevolent as they are experienced, direct the young people in their work; they give them advice, showing them what it is necessary to do in order to work well, and gradually initiating them into all the difficulties of the profession.

Thanks to that education, as paternal as it is practical, the apprentices make rapid progress. No longer wasting time, as before, in attending lectures or carrying out some detail of the trade, always the same, but being, on the contrary, carefully educated in during everything concerned with their profession, they learn the most difficult jobs in two or three years and emerge from the model workshops already good and very capable workers, quite capable of earning their living in private industry.

These establishments of apprenticeship are rather costly to the Government, by virtue of the expense of their installation, and especially because of the time that the workers spend giving lessons to the young apprentices, but the Administration does not regret that expense and, on the contrary, deems it to be very fruitful, a country being more prosperous as good workers become more numerous there and more skilled in their trades.

For apprenticeships in Commerce and heavy industry, the State has no need to create model workshops. The young people destined for those professions simply enter large Government shops and factories, where they are instructed paternally and directed by individuals specially charged with that responsibility. Thanks to those excellent lessons, after a certain time, they can make themselves useful, and do not take long to acquire a place among the employees and draw a wage.

Finally, for the so-called liberal professions, which require theoretical knowledge and special skills, specialist schools have been created in which young people are carefully instructed in everything that they need to know. These include:

The School of Highways-and-Bridges, where engineers are trained to build roads, bridges, railways and canals.

The School of Mining, from which engineers emerge destined to supervise the work of mines and direct all the large factories belonging to the state.

The Naval School, where people learn to build and navigate ships.

The Schools of Painting, Architecture and Music, which train painters, architects and musicians.

The Schools of Education, which furnish teachers of both sexes to schools and professors for higher education.

The School of Medicine, designed to train physicians.

Finally, the School of Administration, in which the laws of the country and political economy are studied, and in which students are prepared to follow administrative careers.

Expressly omitted from the list have been schools of law and military arts, schools of that sort having become unnecessary in the Republic by virtue of the simplification of the law and the suppression of armies.

Entrance into the various establishments of apprenticeship does not take place at hazard and on the mere request of young people or their parents, but, before being admitted into them, it is necessary to undergo examinations proving that one has the aptitude to follow the career for which one is intended. Thus, for certain trades, great muscular strength is required; for others, a great deal of dexterity; for others, excellent eyesight; for others, an open mind; for yet others, certain scientific or artistic aptitudes.

Naturally, in a question as important as the choice of a career, one must take full account of the level of education possessed by the young people. Those who have never been able to get into the higher schools have no claim to an apprenticeship in a liberal profession and are obliged to fall back on commerce or industry. In the same way, those who have not been able to win admission into the secondary schools are forbidden certain professions reserved for their more intelligent and more studious comrades. Equality is in no way compromised by that, because, on the one hand, all children being subjected to the same examinations, those who cannot pass them appropriately cannot blame anyone but themselves for that, and, on the other hand, the young people who embrace careers in commerce and industry have little reason to complain, being able to acquire, with activity and intelligence, a social position equivalent to any liberal profession.

The Government does not limit itself to checking whether young people have real aptitudes for the positions for which they are destined, but determines the number of apprentices to be recruited to each industry. That regulation of apprenticeship has seemed totally indispensable to ensure the prosperity of the country and enable everyone to be able to live comfortably by exercising the trade they have been taught.

Previously, under the old regime, when apprenticeship was not subject to any regulation and young people chose their profession at hazard, this is what happened:

Certain professions, reputed to be good or easy to learn, were oversubscribed and could not nourish all those exercising them. There would, therefore, be frenzied competition between workers of a particular sort, which inevitably led to a lowering of wages, unemployment and poverty. The workers tried in vain to associate, in order to maintain prices; individual self-interest as more powerful and the unemployed workers always offered to work more cheaply than the tariffs imposed by strikes.

With the efficient organization of apprenticeship established by the Social Republic, similar economic disorder is not longer to be feared. A statistical committee, made up of experts, procures all the necessary information and calculates every year what the needs of industry are, and consequently fixes the number of apprentices to be taken on in each employment.

The sales records of commercial establishments and the tax records permit the relevant labor statistics to be determined with great exactitude, and when a young person has been admitted to a model workshop and has learned a trade there, he is certain on emerging therefrom to find work and to earn a living honorably by exercising the profession to which he has devoted himself.

## 6. Adult Education and Academies

In all large cities, the Government has instituted public lecture courses that students follow, and with which adults can improve their education. These lectures, given by the most distinguished professors, embrace the totality of information: literature, languages both dead and alive, natural history, medicine, physics, chemistry, astronomy, mathematics, etc. The lessons take place in the day and also in the evenings, in order that workers can attend without missing work. Although the lecture theaters in which the lessons are held are immense, they are always filled with a numerous crowd, so great is the merit of the professors and the zeal of the population.

Not content with having instituted these public courses, the Government has encouraged open education and puts the State lecture theaters at the disposal of citizens who want to deliver lectures on any subject whatsoever. There are writers who treat literary matters, travelers who give accounts of their voyages, scientists who reveal new discoveries, and so on. Nothing is more varied and instructive than these individual lectures, and, although the improvised professors are not always very eloquent, they rarely fail to attract a fairly numerous audience.

Another kind of instruction that the Government has not neglected is that provided by public libraries. There is one in every city. Classic works can be found there, as well as many other useful or curious books that one can read within the library or take home for a few days.

As well as public libraries, there are reading-rooms everywhere, in which all of modern literature, contemporary books and newspapers can be read. These reading-rooms are considered to be commercial establishments and are run by Government employees. They are not free, but the cost of a subscription or a reading session is minimal, the Administration drawing no profit from it and often making a loss. It is consoled by the thought that the education of the people always brings back more than it costs, and that it is still better to read a bad book than get drunk in some dirty tavern.

For their part, individuals, rivaling the Government in their zeal for education, have formed a multitude of scientific, literary and artistic societies, embracing the entire extent of human knowledge. Thus, in all cities, even the smallest, there are societies of agriculture, meteorology, botany and archaeology, choral societies and brass bands, etc.

All these free associations correspond with one another; they communicate their work and hold meetings for competitions. Whenever they fulfill a genuinely useful function, the Administration does not fail to encourage them and accord them subsidies to buy instruments or publish their proceedings.

One of those societies is classified among the establishments of public utility and has become a veritable

State institution. I am referring to the Academy of Paris, which unites in its bosom all the illustrious individuals in France, in literary or scientific terms. That society, famous throughout the entire world, had five hundred full members, divided into five specialized Academies, each with a hundred members, to wit:

The Academy of Belles-Lettres, for poets, dramatists, novelists, journalists and other writers.

The Academy of Fine Arts, for painters, sculptors, engravers, architects and musicians.

The Academy of Literary Sciences, for historians, economists, philosophers, archeologists, philologists, etc.

The Academy of Natural Sciences, for anatomy, physiology, medicine, botany, zoology, geology, meteorology, etc.

Finally, the Academy of Exact Sciences, for physics, chemistry, astronomy and mathematics.

The members of these various academies are not elected by the academicians, as was the case under the old regime, but are elected by the Parisians themselves with the aid of universal suffrage and a majority vote.

That kind of election had the result of suppressing intrigue and favor, and of only bringing into the Institute people who have made a name through their works. This has significantly changed the composition of two academies, those of Belle-Lettres and Fine Arts.

One the one hand, a certain number of female artists and authors have been elected, to whom academic chairs were previously rigorously refused. On the other hand, the vote of Parisians has sent into these learned assemblies specialties that would once have seemed out of place. Thus, the Academy of Belles-Lettres counts many novelists and journalists among its numbers, and a few talented actors and actresses. Similarly, places in the Academy of Fine Arts have been gives to photographers of merit, instrumentalists, and singers of both sexes, alongside painters and composers of music.

In spite of all the errors that universal suffrage might commit, the Academicians' places are nonetheless avidly sought by talented people, and they are the obligatory consecration of all literary or scientific renown. Thus, the Government has a great deal of consideration for those who have succeeded in being elected; it allows them a salary of twelve thousand francs, and thus puts them among the number of the richest citizens of the Social Republic.

# V. GOVERNMENT

## 1. Legislative Power

The Government of the Social Republic is constituted by two distinct powers, which have clearly separate attributions: the legislative power, which makes the
will of the People known and formulates it in laws; and
the executive power, which implements the laws voted
by the legislators.

These two powers have a common origin, however,
in universal suffrage. The people composing them are all
elected directly by the vote of their fellow citizens and
are thus merely the delegates of the People, who are and
remain the veritably sovereign.

Citizens all have the right to vote as soon as they
reach the age of majority at eighteen, and can only be
deprived of it by a decision of a court when they have
broken the law of the land. Women are not allowed to
vote but they obtain their revenge by using their influence to direct the votes of their husbands, relatives and
acquaintances—and in fact, although they do not participate in the count, it is they who determine elections and
choose all the members if the Government.

Elections for the legislative body take place every
year and are carried out in the following manner.

Within each electoral constituency, the citizens vote
by open ballot for the candidates of their choice. When
one of them has gathered a thousand votes in that fashion he is declared elected and people immediately cease

voting for him. As for the candidates who have less than a thousand votes at the end of the count, they are submitted to second ballots until the most fortunate has obtained a sufficient number of votes to be elected. Finally, if, after the second ballots there are still more than five hundred electors in the constituency who have not elected anyone, those five hundred can select a representative exactly as if they were a thousand.

In sum, the Republic's representatives are appointed by a thousand electors only—electors whose names and addresses they know, with whom they can communicate frequently. It is thus easy for them to consult the sentiments of their electors on every question and vote in accordance.

They never fail to do this, so it can be said that the People are genuinely represented by the legislative body, and when it votes on a law, it is exactly as if the citizens were voting themselves.

Under the old regime, when legislators were appointed by a secret ballot of 35,000 voters, it was very different. In those times, the electors, not being personally known to their representatives, could not communicate with them and thus make known their views on every question. So what happened? The representative acted exactly as they wished, voting according to their own opinions and not that of their electors. Before the election they made the most lavish promises in order to attract the favor of the public, but once elected they forgot them all and scarcely gave any thought to the desires and interests of the citizens they were said to represent.

The representatives of the Social Republic are elected for a year only, but they are indefinitely re-electable, and, if they strive to be worthy of their electors, they are indeed almost always re-elected and maintain their mandate for life.

The representatives receive and appropriate salary from the State, but it is forbidden for them to hold any other employment or exercise any industry for as long as their mandate lasts. Responsible for representing the People, they must devote themselves entirely to that task and consecrate all their time to it. All plurality, of any kind, is thus prohibited, and when the citizens perceive that a representative is negligent in fulfilling his functions and does not devote the necessary time and energy to them, they ceased to vote for him and choose someone more diligent in his stead.

Once elected, the provincial representatives do not come to Paris but remain in their départements, within easy reach of their electors, and go to the local center, where they form a deliberating assembly. These provincial assemblies have exactly the same rights as those elected by the inhabitants of Paris and residing in that city. They all discuss public affairs, vote laws in the general interest and possess to the same degree the legislative power of which they are an integral part.

When it is a matter involving the entire country, the Government submits it to all the French representatives, then counts the votes for and against, and passes or rejects the proposal according to whether the majority has accepted or rejected it. If, on the other hand, it is a matter of purely local legislation, the discussion remains circumscribed within the assembly of the département concerned, and the other legislative bodies are not involved.

Thanks to the mode of election and constitution of the national legislative body, it is an exact representation of the will of the sovereign People and all the decisions it takes are inspired by the general interest and the desire to ensure the prosperity of the country. However, the representatives have other functions that are almost as important as that of making laws. In continuous communication with their electors, they listen to their demands and bring them to the attention of the Government. Thus, when a citizen has a petition to make or believes that he has a complaint against the Administration, he rapidly addresses himself to his representative, who takes it up and speaks on his behalf, exposing his grievances in the Chamber, and gives the matter all the desirable publicity.

On the other hand, when the Government needs to consult public opinion on some matter, it addresses itself to the legislative body and asks it to appoint a committee. The latter immediately opens an enquiry, and its report, which always reflects the true state of minds, serves to align the conduct of the Administration.

A multitude of questions, which would previously have been left to the arbitration of the Authority, are submitted in this manner to the tribunal of public opinion. Far from complaining and regretting its lost attributions, the Government multiplies these enquiries, only too glad thus to diminish its responsibility and to share with others the heavy task of administering a large population and pleasing everyone.

Finally, to ensure the free manifestation of the public opinion of which the legislative body is the official organ, the citizens have complete liberty to come together and to express their thoughts by way of the Press.

Without preliminary authorization and without the surveillance of any commissioner they can hold public meetings and discuss there any questions of religion, politics or social economics. Far from raising any obstacle to these assemblies, the Government favors them by making large and comfortable halls available to the public.

In the Social Republic the Press similarly enjoys complete liberty. There are no deposits or official stamps, and anyone can found a periodical and wrote whatever he likes therein without fear of being subjected to fines or send to prison.

Thanks to that liberty, political newspapers are very numerous, very cheap and yet well-produced. Generally edited by the representatives of the legislative body, who find them a convenient means of putting themselves in daily communication with their electors, they are completely filled with instructive and interesting articles and do not contain a single advertisement.

It is they that genuinely represent public opinion, and as all citizens subscribe to at least one paper and read others in reading-rooms, the People are well acquainted with the country's affairs and really exercise the executive and legislative powers that they delegate to their representatives.

## 2. The Executive Power

Among the Socialists of the year 2000, executive Authority is entrusted to a single magistrate: the Secretary of the Republic.

That Secretary promulgates the laws votes by the legislative body, and is responsible for their execution. He is the head of the Administration, appoints all the employees, either directly or through the intermediary of his ministers, and while, so to speak, doing nothing himself, is solely responsible for all the actions of the Government and must answer to the country for the power placed in his hands.

The Secretary of the Republic is elected by the direct universal suffrage of the whole of France, of which he is the delegate, and which confides to him the exercise of national sovereignty. He is elected by simple majority; moreover, the ballot is secret, in order that everyone may vote freely, without fear of making enemies.

When the Social Republic was proclaimed, it was initially decided that the Secretary would only be appointed for a year and could never be re-elected. This measure was adopted in order to prevent that usurpation of power and not to give it to a master. Soon, however, the Socialists perceived that, in order to avoid one danger, they were falling into a much greater evil: anarchy.

In fact, scarcely had the annual Secretary been elected than people began wondering anxiously, who would be put in his place the following year. There was no lack of candidates, and as soon as one of them appeared to have a greater chance, he was immediately surrounded, adulated and acclaimed. Everyone wanted to be his intimate friend and collaborate in his election, some for fear of losing their positions, others in order to obtain better ones.

In France, therefore there were always two heads of government at once—one in exercise and one in expectation. The latter was no less influential, and his innumerable partisans agitated with the passion of hopeful ambition. In order to put their man in a good light and ensure his election, they mounted a systematic opposition to the Authority, indiscriminately criticizing all the Administration's decisions and repeating at every opportunity that France would never be happy until the candidate of their choice had been elected.

Once elected, he new Secretary began by dismissing all the employees who had not rallied to his candidature with sufficient rapidity, and giving their positions to the devoted partisans to whom he owed his election. Then he tried to keep his promises and to occupy himself with the country's affairs, but was impeded in his turn by a new candidate for the Secretariat, who soon became the leader of a powerful opposition and began a new electoral campaign as agitated as that of the preceding year.

In addition to that, the Secretaries being unable ever to be re-elected, it was soon necessary to take men of little or no ability, and when, by chance, an intelligent administrator appeared who handled the Republic's affairs well, at the end of the year it was necessary to bid him farewell like all the rest and replace him with someone less competent.

Things proceeded in this fashion for some time, but as disorder and agitation increased continually, the Socialists ended up getting weary of that anarchy and decided to amend their Constitution. They declared than in future, the Secretary of the Republic would be appointed for ten years, and that he could be re-elected at the expiry of his mandate. That long delegation of power ceased immediately, of course, and before the fixed term, in case of crime, madness grave infirmity or notorious incapability. In all such circumstances, the legislative body had to vote a law calling upon the people, who had to vote yes or no as to whether the Secretary in office was to retain or quit his position.

As soon as a decennial Secretary was appointed who was very capable, agitation and anxiety ceased, to give way to confidence and security. He engaged in a little less politics, but paid much more attention to his own duties, and employees and manufacturers, instead of thinking about changing the Government, no longer thought about anything but getting down to work and fulfilling their functions. The Administration, no longer being hindered by a noisy opposition, put all its zeal into choosing its functionaries and giving advancement not to the most conspiratorial but to the most capable. The Authority, reassured of it future and certain of achieving what it had begun, undertook immense projects of public utility, and was able to bring them to completion.

In brief, after ten years of general prosperity and perfect tranquility, the people were so satisfied with his regime and were so unworried about possible usurpation that they reelected the same Secretary and entrusted him with a new mandate. Only a few extreme Republicans were discontented. They said that liberty had been lost, that the Government was no longer a Republic but a Monarchy, and that, at that price, France would pay dearly for the wellbeing it enjoyed. But France let them speak, and, whether it was a Republic or an elective Monarchy, the Constitution it had adopted satisfied it, and it had no desire to change it.

Below the Secretary of the Republic are the Ministers, appointed by him and each responsible for a major public service.

These Ministers, nine in number, are:

The Minister of the Interior, who appoints the commissioners of the départements and the mayors of the communes, commands the public force and answers for the maintenance of order.

The Minister of Finance, who oversees taxation, directs the National Bank, collects the State's receipts and pays all its expenses.

The Minister of Public Education, who is responsible for schools, libraries, scientific and literary societies, the Academy and so on.

The Minister of Justice, who appoints judges and makes sure that they fulfill their duties efficiently.

The Minister of Public Works, whose department is responsible for the houses and monuments belonging to the State, for letting them, repairing them and constructing new ones.

The Minister of Transport, whose responsibilities include roads, canals and railways as well as the transportation of goods, passengers, letters and telegraphic dispatches.

The Minister of Marine, who presides over the construction of ships and maritime navigation.

The Minister of Industry, who directs the metallurgical establishments and various factories belonging to the State.

The Minister of Commerce, who has the employees of retail and wholesale stores under his orders, and is responsible for the purchase and sake of merchandise.

Finally, there is one other ministry, the Secretariat, which has no minister of its own but is under the direct control of the Secretary of the Republic, whose responsibilities are rather complicated; it promulgates the laws, maintains relations with foreign powers, distributed national rewards and presides over all the ceremonies of the socialist religion.

### 3. Public Force

The executive Authority of the Republic does not have at its disposal any permanent army, national or mobile guard. The only public force it possesses consists of a few gendarmes and police agents responsible for maintaining order and supervising the execution of the law.

That radical suppression of permanent armies, and hence of all civil or foreign wars, is not the least benefit that the Socialists have rendered to humankind. That was one of their first reforms, and it is curious to relate how they went about establishing permanent peace between peoples and putting an end to the ruinous armaments that were exhausting the finances of all States.

As soon as the Socialist Government was solidly established, it proposed a general disarmament to all the neighboring Powers. To that effect, it selected the men most highly recommended by their knowledge and eloquence, and dispatched them as ambassadors to the various sovereigns.

The latter could not have given a better welcome to the Republic's envoys; they listened very attentively to their harangues regarding the horrors of war and the benefits of peace, and never failed to applaud the finest passages warmly. Then they replied that all the sentiments of fraternity expressed by the ambassadors were worthy of praise, but that they were totally impractical; to their great regret, and in order to safeguard the honor and security of their people, they were therefore obliged to keep their permanent armies and to undertake a small war every now and again in order to permit their officers to win promotion.

The French envoys returned disappointed, but the Government did not lose hope of convincing the foreign princes and clearly demonstrating to them the advantages of peace.

The new diplomats chosen for the second mission were neither very knowledgeable nor very eloquent. The majority of them expressed themselves quite incorrectly—some did not even know how to read—but their number, there being twelve hundred thousand of them, substituted perfectly for their lack of education. Clad simply in red trousers and gray coats, with knapsacks on their backs, equipped with advanced weapons, they went to pay visits to neighboring kings, singing the verses of the *Marseillaise* to amuse themselves.

For their part, the sovereigns of Europe came to an understanding between themselves, and in order to receive us worthily, they also chose a large number of ambassadors similar to ours, except that their uniforms were different. The two diplomatic processions met in the middle of a vast plain, and, without further ceremony, they immediately made contact and set about exchanging explanations.

First, the French envoys began by presenting a series of preliminary notes consisting of cannonballs and rifle-bullets—notes that immediately convinced and reduced to silence all those who took cognizance of them. The foreign kings, however, observed that these arguments were already very old, obsolete, and told them nothing knew about the inconvenience of pitched battles.

Our ambassadors agreed, in fact, that that kind of reasoning was quite old and that much better ones had recently been discovered. To provide proof of that, they immediately dispatched a considerable number of protocols consisting of explosive shells and bullets. These protocols were no longer addressed to isolated individuals but to entire companies, from which they removed any desire ever to deliver themselves to any combat.

The allied Princes got a good taste of the spirit and detail of these protocols and began to admit that war was a horrible thing and that peace was greatly preferable. They still retained numerous doubts, however. The French took responsibility for dissipating every last one of those doubts with irresistible ultimatums. These were rockets loaded with potassium picrate—rockets that enveloped an entire regiment in a furnace of flaming gases and reduced all the soldiers to little pieces of charcoal.[8]

When they had witnessed the sending of these ultimatums, which were carefully repeated several times over, the allied kings were gripped with a profound horror of war and an inexpressible enthusiasm for the mildness of peace. They immediately declared that ideas of universal fraternity were the most practical in the world. Not only did they immediately renounce the maintenance of permanent armies, but, resigning voluntarily from their sovereignty, they established Republican Government in their own countries, and in order to set a personal example of the solidarity of peoples, they went to live abroad as simple individuals.

On their departure, they only made one reproach to the French—that they had not sent the second embassy, whose arguments had been so successful, first.

"There," they said, pointing to the envoys in red trousers, "are practical and eloquent orators, who know

---

[8] Although potassium picrate had first been prepared in the 17th century it only began commercial manufacture and routine use in 1869 and must have been the "latest thing" when Moilin wrote this novella; he was therefore not in a position to know that, although it is indeed a powerful explosive, potassium picrate would prove impractical for military use and would instead be virtually confined in its applications to fireworks. The world would have to wait some time for the development of *fusées* [rockets]—or, more exactly, guided missiles—capable of having the effect that Moilin describes here. He was neither the first nor the last writer of futuristic fiction to take it for granted that warfare would have to be abandoned once sufficiently powerful weapons were developed, and could not know what a horrible error that was.

how to make what they have to say understood, and we like them a thousand times better than your first ambassadors, who talked for hours on end, and proved absolutely nothing."

## 4. Taxes

In the Social Republic of the year 2000, the returns of taxation are considerable, reaching approximates ten billion francs. That figure is not at all exorbitant, however, if one considers the number and the extent of the public services maintained by the State and the multitude of its employees.

In fact, in Socialist society, save for Agriculture and light industry, left to individual initiative, it is the Government that does absolutely everything. It provides Education, distributed Credit, constructs houses, railways, roads, canals, charters ships and controls Commerce. Now, it is easy to comprehend that to do all that requires a great deal of money, and that ten billion is really not excessive. In any case, in spite of the magnitude of the figure, taxation seems light to individuals because it is always equitably distributed and never falls upon the necessary, but is addressed solely to the superfluous.

The Social Republic's taxes are not every numerous, but are very productive. They are:

Firstly, income tax, as we have already mentioned. It is proportional to annual income so long as that does not exceed twelve thousand francs, but above that figure it becomes total and takes into the public Treasury everything in excess of the legal maximum.

Many manufacturers, far from limiting their business when they have earned an income of twelve thousand francs, make it even more extensive and have the honor of making large profits in order to remit them to the State. That conduct is not as disinterested as it appears, because it wins them a great deal of consideration and influence, and makes them important people. Moreover, the Government can express its gratitude to these voluntary tax-collectors; it often honors them with national rewards and willingly appoints them to much sought-after positions as experts attached to tribunals.

On the other hand, the social position of citizens, the value of their retirement pensions and the aid given to them by the State are based on the income that they declare themselves to have. Everyone, by virtue of self-esteem, and also of self-interest, therefore exaggerates his wealth rather than minimizing it, and a considerable number of people pay more to the State than they need to, with the sole objective of passing themselves off as being richer than they really are.

All these causes, in combination, ensure that the income tax is extremely productive and one of the Treasury's best resources.

In any case, if manufacturers were tempted to understate the figure of their annual income, the Government would perceive it immediately, for, buying everything from and selling everything to individuals, it knows everyone's annual expenditure to the nearest centime. That sort of verification is not applicable, however, to physicians and other professionals who do not sell anything to the State, and deal directly with the public. In order to calculate the exact income of those citizens, the Administration takes charge of collecting all fees on their behalf. Far from complaining, physicians are strongly in favor of that measure, only too glad to receive their fees without having any need to occupy themselves with questions of money, so repugnant to a liberal mind.

Secondly, the tax on Credit. We have already seen that the National Bank lends to all manufacturers who are in need, so long as they can offer guarantees of reimbursement. Although the interest on the sums advanced is minimal and not at all usurious, it produces a considerable annual profit, which covers all the expenses of administration and contributes about two billion to the State coffers.

Thirdly, sales taxes. All the Republic's commerce beings in the hands of the Government, the profits that result therefrom belong to the State and serve to pay for public expenditure.

The profits made on the sale of merchandise are very variable and depend on the nature of the objects sold. Thus, it is almost zero on all goods of primary necessity, such as common foodstuffs, basic clothing, ordinary wines, cheap furniture, salt, fuel, soap, lighting, etc. It is the same for all the principal raw materials employed by Industry: metals, wood, marble, chemical products, etc., as well as machinery, agricultural implements, books, newspapers, etc.

By contrast, the profits realized on sales are quite considerable for all luxury items and those purchased without any necessity, such as tobacco, strong liquors, fine wines, luxurious furniture, fine fabrics, fashionable and whimsical articles, etc. On all these objects, the Government seeks, without any scruple, to make as much money as possible and to raise prices to the limit at which they will produce the largest benefits without harming consumption. And no one can complain about that measure in buying any item that is unnecessary or nearly so, having the money to do so and being, in consequence, able to pay the tax without inconvenience.

Fourthly, the tax on rents. As previously stated, the Sate owns all the houses in cities and rents them to the citizens. Now these rents, solely by virtue of the competition of individuals, produce handsome annual returns. These, in any case, serve in large measure either for the construction of new houses or for the decoration of those that already exist, and other public services obtain little benefit from that source of revenue.

Fifthly, land tax. This very moderate tax is calculated in the following manner. It is proportional to the extent of the land possessed by each agriculturalist, without taking any account of whether the yield of the land is good or poor, whether it is covered with buildings or left to lie fallow.

This action has been taken with the aim of favoring the progress of Agriculture. The peasant, paying as much for a poor patch of land as for a good one, for terrain that is built on or not, is keenly interest in improving his yields and constructing the necessary buildings. Instead of competing to determine who owns the largest domains, agriculturalists compete in the efficiency of their cultivation. When they own heath-lands or marsh-lands they clear them or drain them, or sell them to someone else who will take responsibility for those operations. If they sometimes give up uncultivated land in order not to pay the tax on it, the State immediately takes possession of it and makes use of it by planting trees.

Another tax has also been established in order to prevent the extreme subdivision of heritages. It is a tax that is collected very time a field is divided and an adjustment to the land-register is requested, although a similar adjustment costs nothing when several parcels of land are combined. In order not to pay that registry tax, families have abandoned their old habit of dividing up inherited land in such a way that some fields are no longer more than a couple of furrows wide, to the great detriment of their crops.

Such are the taxes that exist in the Social Republic. The Administration has often been asked to create new resources with the aid of taxes on windows and doors, on the stamping of official documents and newspapers, on public Education, on imports and exports, on the transport of letters, merchandise and passengers, etc., but the Government has always refused, those sources of revenue seeming to be injurious to the prosperity of the country. If it needs to balance its budget, it prefers to increase one of the five existing taxes slightly rather than establishing a sixth.

## 5. The Law

*Civil Law.*

All Socialist institutions have the objective of obtaining justice between citizens and this preventing protests and lawsuits. It follows that complaints to the courts are very rare in France in the year 2000, and if they have not disappeared completely, it is because there are people who want make a case regardless of merit, who and require to be judged and punished.

Thanks to the small number and scant importance of lawsuits, the judiciary system of the Republic is very simple. It has dispensed entirely with bailiffs, clerks, solicitors, advocates, notaries and the flood of stamped documents that they inscribed. Preliminary Tribunals, Courts of Appeal and Courts of Cassation have similarly been abolished, and that entire costly legal apparatus has been easily replaced by simple Justices of the Peace sitting in every district.

These Justices of the Peace, assisted solely by a secretary, examine and settle all disputes between inhabitants, and do it without files, wads of papers, contradictory speeches and other unnecessary formalities, which have never rendered a judgment more equitable and were only instituted in the interests of lawyers. When a judge needs information about specialized matters, he appoints experts, who make a report and give the court the required elements of appreciation.

When an issue is of sufficient magnitude, and the loser believes that he is in the right, it might be necessary for the initial judgment to be revised by a second justice of the peace known as an appellant. These further judges, of consummate experience and irreproachable integrity, only sit in large cities. They examine the cases submitted to their jurisdiction with the greatest care and render definitive decisions.

When the loser thinks that the law is obscure or that it has been misapplied, however, he can make a further appeal, but only with regard to the interpretation of the law and not the facts of the case. That further appeal take place before the legislative body, perfectly competent in that matter since it makes all the laws of the land and knows better than anyone else the veritable meaning of texts found to be obscure.

*Criminal law.*

Free and obligatory education, which has dissipated ignorance, the organization of labor, which has suppressed poverty, and the laws regarding marriage and inheritance, which have banished domestic hatreds, have all greatly reduced the number of contraventions and crimes. Even in the Republic of the year 2000, however, some are committed, and this is how they are judged and punished.

Those who are guilty of assaults inflicting trivial injuries, insults, and calumnious imputations against individuals or Government employees, contraventions of regulations and other similar actions are brought before a so-called police magistrate.

The latter, aided by his secretary, examines the affair, hears witnesses, and then renders a reasoned verdict in public. The penalties he applies are only of two kinds: fines and the deprivation of civil rights. Imprisonment has been abandoned, which, as well as costing the State dearly, prevents the sentenced individual from working and thus harms he prosperity of the nation. As for the deprivation of civil rights, it is applied very frequently. That punishment, although entirely moral, is greatly feared by citizens, who are anxious to conserve their right to vote and, in consequence, do not take the risk of having it withdrawn. In any case, the deprivation of civil rights is usually only pronounced for the duration of a year, except in cases of recidivism, when the court is more severe.

Crimes and misdemeanors—fraud, theft, perjury, serious assault, attempted murder, murder, rape, poisoning, etc.—are tried in the Court of Assizes.

Once, under the old regime, these various crimes were quite common. They were almost all committed by a category of individuals, always the same, who were at war with society and spent half their lives in prison and the other half meriting their return thereto. Far from reforming the guilty, penitentiaries and prisons only rendered them more audacious and more skillful; they were veritable schools of crime—schools that were also very costly to the Administration. The death penalty was available against major criminals, but juries found it repellent and it was rarely requested—and, in addition, every execution was even more costly than imprisonment.

The Socialist Government, at its inception, did not hesitate for an instant in changing the punishments applied to crimes. It abolished imprisonment, forced labor and the death penalty, and replaced them with a single punishment: deportation for life to Algeria or Guyana, according to the seriousness of the crime.

Deportation to Algeria is not, strictly speaking, true deportation, but rather a means of rapidly colonizing that beautiful country. The exiles who are sent there are not subjected to any surveillance, and can exercise their professions freely. As the acts they have committed are sufficiently pardonable, they are made welcome by the Arab populations, who are not afflicted with any great honesty themselves, and, as is well-known, practice theft and murder on a grand scale.

Thanks to their industry and intelligence, the deportees placed in that new environment rapidly succeed in gathering possessions, and then, far from thinking of stealing from others, think of nothing but defending their wealth and their lives against the attacks of the indigenes. Among the Arabs, however, punishments are more severe than in France, and, although futile and costly prisons have been abolished there, the death penalty has been retained and is frequently applied.

In a few years, that emigration of citizens sentenced by our courts had made Algeria a truly French territory, as prosperous in its agriculture as its industry, where no more crimes were committed than under the old regime. For its part, carefully expurgated of all the inhabitants who did not want to comply with its laws, France has become the most honest country in the world; crimes are becoming rarer there every day, and it is hoped that they might one day disappear entirely, and the courts can be abolished.

Deportation to Guyana is imposed on all individuals guilty of serious and infamous crimes.

Once they have arrived at their destination, the deportees are closely supervised to begin with, and then, if their conduct is satisfactory, they are released. Then they establish themselves in the country, working at their profession, marrying between themselves, and, if their own rehabilitation is never complete, at least their children can become honest citizens and contribute to the prosperity of the colony.

As for hardened criminals who do not want to behave decently, they are treated as furious lunatics and kept locked up until they die.

But let us return to the assize courts that judge crimes. Each of them is composed of ten jurors chosen by lot and by a criminal magistrate who directs the discussion, interrogates the accused and the witnesses and passes sentence.

That judge, aided by his secretary, first examines the case, determines whether there are grounds to continue, and assembles the elements of the evidence. Two Government advocates are charged, one with presenting the defense of the accused, the other with demonstrating his guilt. These two advocates are absolutely equal in rank and prerogatives, and if the tribunal makes any allowances, they are for the defense.

After the interrogation of the accused, hearing the witnesses and the advocates' speeches, the jury confers and renders its verdict, and the judge, applying the law as read, pronounces a sentence in conformity with the jury's decision. Accused persons found not guilty are immediately set free and the others are expelled from France forever and must spend the rest of their lives either in Algeria or Guyana.

## 6. National Rewards

Although the Government strives to render the necessity of punishing the guilty rarer, it multiplies, by contrast, opportunities to provide national rewards to those who merit them.

These national rewards are very numerous.

To begin with, there are prizes that are distributed every year to young pupils who have distinguished themselves by their application and their success in examinations. These sorts of prizes are of great importance, and the Minister of Public Education makes sure that they are awarded with the most scrupulous impartiality. Not only do they reward the work of studious children and encourage them to persist in their efforts, but they are useful to young people subsequently, when it is a matter of finding positions and making use of their aptitudes in some profession or other.

The prizes that are given out in schools are, therefore, serious national rewards, and are considered as such by the pupils. In order to acquire them, the students work ardently all year, and hold in high esteem those who obtain considerable success, regarding them as their natural leaders.

National rewards have similarly been instituted in the model workshops, which are distributed every year to young apprentices who have attracted attention by the assiduity of their work and the precocity of their skills.

These apprenticeship prizes are preciously-worked tools of honor, engraved with the names of those who have obtained them.

When young people have become working adults, the Government still continues to treat them as children and reward their hard work and intelligence, except that the prizes given change their form, and it is no longer books or tools that are awarded to the winners but gold, silver and bronze medals.

Every year, in each département, competitions and exhibitions are held for all the products of Industry, Agriculture and Fine Arts. Committees appointed by the legislative body examine all the exhibited objects attentively and assess the value of new inventions. Above all, they carefully investigate who really deserves credit for products judged worth of recompense—whether it is the employer, the worker, or both, and he medals are awarded in consequence. Thus, simple artisans and modest cultivators frequently win national rewards, of which they are extremely proud, because they testify to their skill and place them above their undecorated comrades.

In addition to départemental exhibitions, there is an annual general competition in Paris for one of the branches of Industry: furniture, clothing, metalwork, livestock, cereals, etc. Only those who have already been awarded medals by their départements are admitted to these competitions. The winners are given large so-called medals of honor , much sought after because they put those who obtain them at the head of French labor.

There are acts of devotion and courage that merit national rewards, even though those who have performed them have acted with the purest disinterest. Committees drawn from the legislative body are charged with seeking out all the citizens who have distinguished themselves by some heroic action and awarding them special medals, which they attach to their chests in such a manner as to put their personal courage in evidence.

Of all these national rewards, however, the one that is most sought after and most highly esteemed, the one that everyone desires to have, is the award known as "the Republic."

It is a little golden jewel representing the image of the Republic, which can easily be worn on the body by attaching it with a red ribbon. That jewel serves to reward all those citizens who have been a credit to the fatherland and have distinguished themselves either by some work of striking merit or by long devotion to the public interest. Like all the other national rewards, it is awarded indistinctly to males and females. The only difference is that the latter always wear the jewel itself, of which they make an ornament, while the former content themselves with a simple red ribbon, unless they are in ceremonial dress.

In order further to reward those who have obtained the Republic but have nevertheless continue to distinguish themselves, several kinds of decorations have been created that are added to the jewel itself, which is ornamented to varying degrees with precious stones, and also to the ribbon, which is knotted into a variously complicated rosette. Thus, there are five classes of Republics, which can only be obtained successively, by giving proof of ever-greater merit.

The Government makes sure that the national reward of the Republic is distributed with scrupulous equity, and one can say with good reason that it is awarded by public opinion itself.

Every year, the legislative body appoints committees to determine who the citizens are who merit being decorated; then the comparative merits of the candidates is discussed in open session, and a definitive list is drawn up, which is presented to the Government. The latter, when it gives the Republic to someone, is merely ratifying the choice expressed by the country's representatives, so the decoration is envied beyond all expression, and to obtain it, citizens devoted themselves to the most stubborn labors, competing in devotion to the public good.

A few stern individuals have, however, criticized national rewards in general and the Republic in particular. They claim that rewarding citizens when they have done well is treating them like children, and that true Republicans have no need of such encouragements to be virtuous, being content with the intimate testimony of their conscience. The Government agrees entirely with that opinion, but unfortunately, in France in the year 200 there are very few "true" Republicans and a great many ordinary Republicans. The Administration is therefore obliged to conform to the tastes of the majority and persists in decorating all the citizens who merit it.

# VI. RELIGION AND CUSTOMS

## 1. Baptism

The French of the year 2000 profess the greatest religious tolerance, and everyone among them is free to follow whatever religion they please, or none at all if they think that more appropriate. However, the overwhelming majority of citizens practice the so-called socialist or civil religion, which is that of the State and is officially professed by the members of the Government.

That socialist religion is, in any case, extremely simple. It consists solely of surrounding with pomp and all the apparatus of public power the four great circumstances of life: birth, coming of age, marriage and death.

*Socialist baptism.*

As soon as a child comes into the world, the parents must notify the officer of the civil estate and have the new-born's birth certificate drawn up. That formality is obligatory for all citizens, no matter what religion they practice. Socialists, however, only make a provisional declaration of birth and reserve the official declaration for a little later, when the mother has recovered sufficiently to take part in the ceremony, and the child has been vaccinated and is strong enough to be transported without inconvenience. It is usually at the age of six months that the official presentation takes place, to which common parlance has given the named of socialist baptism, even though no ablution is involved.

On the day chosen for the solemnity, the parents of the new-born gather their family, friends and acquaintances and then, dressed in their best clothes, they take the metropolitan railway and go in a procession to the socialist Temple. That Temple, it will be remembered, is situated in the Cité, at the center of the International Palace. In the aisle to the left of the entrance are a number of large chapels exclusively devoted to the baptism of young Socialists and, in consequence, ornamented with paintings and statues recalling the principal scenes of maternity and infancy.

As soon as the child's parents and their friends have taken their places in the chapel assigned to them, a second procession arrives of magistrates charged with presiding over the baptism—magistrates who are delegated by the Secretary of the Republic and occupy the highest rank in the State. The members of this new procession take their places in the choir-stalls of the chapel and the ceremony begins.

First the parents take the child and come forward, accompanied by four witnesses. They present the infant, declaring its sex, indicating the day and time of its birth and the names they wish to bestow upon it.

Once the declaration of birth is concluded, the parents and their witnesses take turns to promise solemnly to bring up the new-born in the principles of Socialism, never to make it perform any exercise of any other religion, not to teach it any prayers or any catechism, and not to allow it to witness the rites of other religions except by way of a spectacle. That promise is inscribed in the Temple registers, then signed by the witnesses, and is always faithfully kept by the parents, who would be dishonored if they broke such a solemn engagement.

Immediately after the swearing of the oath, one of the magistrates goes up into the pulpit and makes a speech appropriate to the occasion. He talks about the care and affection owed to children, the names given to the new-born, the lives of famous individuals who have borne the same names, the beauty of the socialist religion and its immense superiority by comparison with other religions, etc. That harangue lasts for some time, and, as it is always made by an excellent orator, many strangers come to watch socialist baptisms out of simple curiosity and without knowing the family of the baptized child.

When the orator has concluded his speech, another magistrate—the same one who presided over the solemnity—speaks in his turn. In the name of the entire nation he adopts the new-born, recognizes it as a Socialist, and promises to watch carefully over its life, its education and its future. At the same time, he gives the parents a little gold medal, on which are engraved the child's names and date of birth. That medal is immediately put around the young Socialist's neck, and the latter will not remove it until the age of majority.

The handing over of the medal concludes the ceremony; the magistrates withdraw in single file, the child's cortege returns to the parents' domicile, and they day concludes with a dinner party, at which the newly-baptized child is welcomed and celebrated, by drinking to its health.

## 2. Coming of Age

When children baptized as Socialists reach the age of majority, they take part in a further ceremony, in which they confirm the promise made at their birth and engage on their own behalf to profess the national religion and not to practice any other religion.

In order to be admitted to a celebration of one's coming of age it is not sufficient to reach the age of eighteen. It is also necessary for young men and young women to know and fulfill all the duties of a good Socialist, that their masters be satisfied with their work and their conduct, and, in sum, that they are found worthy to enter the religious society of which they desire to be a part. To be judged unworthy and set back until the following year is considered very shameful, so all young people as they approach the end of their eighteenth year, become models of virtue, so fearful are they of acquiring a black mark and not being authorized to celebrate their coming of age.

The solemnity in question normally takes place on the anniversary of their birth. On that day, the neophytes put on a special and official costume, which is very simple—entirely black for males and entirely white for females—and then, accompanied by their parents and friends from school or workshop, go in procession to the international Temple.

There, to the right of the monument, are special chapels designed, some for young men and the others for young women, and decorated in consequence with paintings and bas-relief representing the work and duties of one or other sex.

It is in one of these chapels that a ceremony takes place loosely resembling the one of baptism. In the presence of magistrates of the Republic and numerous witnesses drawn by curiosity, the novices give their names and ages, furnish evidence of good conduct and show testimonials from their masters; then the parents and witnesses to the baptism come forward to affirm that they have been brought up according to the principles of the socialist religion.

The neophyte then comes forward and makes a solemn promise to persist throughout their life in that same religion, to marry within it, to bring up their children in it, to be buried civilly within it and never to have recourse to any other religions. The neophyte's witnesses, chosen from among older comrades and socialists themselves, corroborate that promise and promise personally to make every effort to maintain their young friend in the religion that has been freely chosen. All these oaths are inscribed in the Temple registers and signed by the people present, and there is no example of their being violated.

An orator then goes up into the pulpit. After a few words about the individual coming of age, the successes thy have achieved in classes or in application to workshop tasks, he explains the duties of youth, the virtues that it ought to present, the happiness and rewards that are reserved for it, and then concludes with a eulogy to the socialist religion and showing how those who profess it are happy and would be wrong o devote themselves to any other religious practices.

After that speech, the magistrate who is presiding over the solemnity speaks in his turn. He declares, in the name of the State, that the neophyte has come of age, that they are free to dispose of their person and their property as they please, and that they may marry, and he invites all the citizens not to treat them as a child any longer but to consider them as a rational adult cognizant of their duties.

Afterwards, if he is male, he is given an elector's card that gives him the right to vote and to participate in the government of the country; if she is female she is similarly given, on behalf of the State, the attributes of the authority exercised by her sex. They are jewelry, such as rings, bracelets, ear-rings, etc. Finally, both receive a concession in the socialist cemetery, and, which is considerably less lugubrious, an invitation to the next ball given in the Cité—a ball at which they will make their so-called entrance into society.

The ceremony is then concluded, and the young adult, accompanied by their relatives and friends, returns home—and the day ends with a cheerful communal dinner, chatting about the ball at which the new citizen will carry out their first adult action, and dance publicly in the Nation's ballroom.

### 3. Marriage

Socialist marriages are celebrated at the International Temple, in a series of chapels situated at the back of the monument. These chapels, which are decorated with every imaginable luxury, are ornamented with paintings representing the joys and duties of marriage: young men courting young women; husbands protecting their wives from danger and devoting themselves to saving their lives; women advising their husbands, steering them away from debauchery and encouraging them always to comport themselves as good citizens; and finally, children completing the happiness of the spouses and further tightening the bonds of affectionate that unite them.

People are only allowed to marry socially when the spouses both profess the socialist religion, and that they have abjured publicly, in the Temple itself, any other religion. These abjurations, which were very numerous when the Socialist Republic was established, took place in the chapels of majority with the ceremonies described in the previous section.

The celebration of marriage is the ceremony to which the socialist religion accords the greatest importance, and the Government has neglected nothing to render it magnificent and surround it with all the prestige of the national authority.

On the day fixed for the solemnity, a special train composed of gala carriages comes to fetch the bride from her home and take her to the wedding at the international Temple. On descending from the carriage, the cortege advances through a curious crowd and, to the sound of music, goes to take its place in one of the nuptial chapels. The magistrates charged with uniting the spouses soon arrive in their turn; they are surrounded by all the paraphernalia of authority, and it is, so to speak, the Republic itself that is coming to preside over and consecrate the marriage of its children.

To begin with, one of the magistrates reads for the final time the banns of the future couple and asks them whether they are unmarried, whether they profess the socialist religion and whether they promise to persist in that religion throughout their lives and bring up their children within it. The couple's eight witnesses then come forward, offer guarantees of that promise and engage solemnly to remind the married couple of it if ever the day comes when they want to abjure the doctrines that they have embraced.

When these preliminaries are complete, an orator goes up to the pulpit. Having said a few words in praise of the two fiancés, he enters into generalities regarding the joys of marriage, the reciprocal duties of spouses, the misfortunes of separations, and concludes by inviting the future couple to remain constantly united and to be models of conjugal life. That speech, always very eloquent, profoundly touches all hearts, especially those of the fiancés, who swear eternal fidelity to one another in hushed voices—an oath too often forgotten, but momentarily sincere.

After that harangue, the magistrate presiding over the ceremony proceeds to marry the spouses. He asks them whether they want to be husband and wife, and whether they promise mutual fidelity and affection. On their affirmative response, he declares them united and hands a certificate to the young woman, while giving the husband a medal on which is engraved the date of the marriage and the names of the two spouses. Then he makes a short paternal speech about the enviable felicities reserved for good wives and faithful husbands.

The marriage concluded, the newly-weds remain in the chapel briefly to receive the congratulations of all their acquaintances, who have come to watch the ceremony. Afterwards, they board the gala train again and head for one of the national residences near Paris, such as Saint-Cloud, Versailles, Meudon, etc.

There, if the weather is fine, the wedding-celebration is held in the gardens; if the weather is bad, it remains inside the apartments. In any case, the residence in question are fitted out in such a way as to offer a thousand distractions to the Government's guests, and the latter can, according to their tastes, swing, play quoits, skittles or billiards, ride donkeys, sail on the lake, refresh themselves at the buffet, etc. All those married on the same day come together in these residences, easily making one another's acquaintance, and these fortuitous encounters between young households often give birth to solid and durable friendships.

However, amid all these amusements, the hour for dinner arrives rapidly. The wedding-feast is provided by the State for the married couple and their cortege, and is served with unusual luxury. In a magnificently-decorated dining-room such as the richest sovereigns never had, a table laden with admirable porcelain, marvelous silverware and sparkling crystal offers the guests an infinite choice of the most delicate dishes and the most renowned wines.

The Government has decided that even the poorest of people should enjoy, at least once in their lives, all the marvels of opulence and all the refinements of civilization, and that the day of their marriage should be marked in their memory as a day of perfect felicity—as wealth, pushed to its utmost limits, is sufficient to give happiness.

The realization of that desire costs the Administration dear, but it is an expense on which no one seeks to skimp, because everyone profits from it, and it encourages marriage, for which Socialists do not have any great propensity. The mere desire to enjoy, once in life, all the terrestrial felicities has caused more than one union to be contracted, and they have not proved to be any less unfortunate than the others.

After having royally celebrated the Government feast and drunk sufficiently to the health of the newlyweds, people leave the table. The men smoke an exquisite cigar, provided by the Nation; the bride and her friends change clothes and put on the ball gowns that they have taken care to bring with them; then they board the gala train again and return to the International Palace. It is there, in the magnificent salons, that the wedding ball is held, to which all the couple's friends and acquaintances in Paris are invited. To the sounds of an enchanting orchestra, the dances go on until dawn, and, sated with pleasures, exhausted by fatigue, falling asleep, the married couple and the guests go home and surrender to the sweetness of repose.

## *4. Burial*

Socialists have a truly incredible religious respect for their dead, and it is astonishing to see a people so light-hearted and incredulous accord so much deference and remembrance to those who are no more. The Government is thus merely in conformity with the mores of the country in surrounding death with a ceremony that is as respectful as it is imposing.

As soon as a citizen has succumbed and the civil estate has been informed of the death by the physician's report, the Administration of funeral ceremonies sends employees to prepare the cadaver and keep vigil beside it. Soon afterwards, the magistrate arrives who is charged with pronouncing the funeral oration of the deceased. He brings together the relatives and friends of the dead person and collects from them all the information necessary to compose his speech. That visit provides a powerful distraction to the grief of the assembly, whose members finds a bitter consolation in remembering the virtues and merits of the individual they have lost.

After the time necessary for the reality of the decease to be fully appreciated, the burial proceeds, and the cadaver is placed in the coffin by the employees of the funeral service. That coffin is exactly the same for all citizens. It is made of simple pine; the coffins of oak and lead, which once established social distinctions even among the dead, have fallen into complete disuse in Socialist society.

As soon as the coffin has been screwed shut and covered with the mortuary cloth, the cortege sets off and goes down into the cellars, where the mourners take a special train on the underground railway. That train, exclusively devoted to funeral service, is comprised of carriages in harmony with that sad destination. It moves at low speed, collecting dead people as it goes brought down from the various quarters through which it passes. Ten similar trains serve the city, and all head for the International Palace, which they reach by going over the Seine bridges, thus arriving in the subterranean sections of the Socialist Temple.

These subterranean workings are disposed in a vast funerary Crypt with lowered vaults, where the blue-tinted light of the funerary lamps seem to thicken the darkness they illuminate. Nothing is as gripping and majestically mournful as the sight of that temple of the dead, where everything has been calculated in order to impose respect and convey the idea of eternal rest. There are no works of art here to attract and delight the eyes, but walls of a depressing nudity and monotony forming galleries of infinite length whose extremities are no longer lit at all and fade away into complete darkness.

No sound from the world of the living reaches these funereal places; a profound silence reigns everywhere, in which the slightest word creates an echo and reverberates fragmentarily along the sonorous vaults. On penetrating into that lugubrious place, one feels seized by a vague terror and, involuntarily, one speaks in hushed tones and walks slowly, fearful of troubling the solemn repose of the silent solitude.

Here and there, mortuary chapels are found, equal in number to the number of people deceased every day. It is in one of those chapels that the funeral service takes place. The coffin is transported there and installed on a catafalque; the audience is arranged around it, and the ceremony begins.

To begin with, the name and occupations of the deceased are announced and the various documents certifying his death are read out. Then the magistrate charged with pronouncing the funeral oration goes up to the pulpit. After having delivered a panegyric to the deceased and spoken about all the inconsolable regrets they have left behind them, the orator enters into generalities regarding the objective of life and the destiny of human beings after death.

In this regard, however, let us say what the philosophical opinions of the Socialists are—opinions that are developed in all funeral orations and furnish an inexhaustible them for the eloquence of preachers.

All Socialists profess the doctrines of pantheistic materialism. They believe that the world is uncreated and eternal, and that it is composed of two profoundly distinct principles, one of them essentially passive and inert, which is matter, the other essentially active and intelligent, which is force.

Reasoning for humans as for the universe, they believe that a human being too is composed of two different principles, one material and passive, which is the body, the other active and intelligent, which is the soul animating the body. After death, they think that the soul and body separate. The former is gradually disorganized; it loses its individuality and is confused with the rest of matter. As for the soul, it is destroyed in the same fashion, stripped of its personality and mingling intimately

130

with the great intelligent All that vivifies the material world.

Socialists are not all in agreement regarding the time necessary to effect the destruction of a soul. Some, the materialists, affirm that the destruction takes place instantaneously, and that, immediately after the last sigh, the mind that animates us evaporates and is lost completely and irrevocably, scattered far and wide within the immensity of Creation. Others, who call themselves spiritualists, believe that the souls of the dead conserve their personality for a long time after death, that they float freely around us, that they can enter into communication with certain individuals or objects, take visible form, pronounce speech, and thus produce all the manifestations attributed to spirits and revenants.

Whatever the existence of spirits might be, it remains the case that Socialists, whether materialist or spiritualist, agree on one important point: the soul is not immortal, and after a lapse of time, whether it be a matter of seconds or years, it loses every last vestige of its individuality and is confused with the great All.

Depending on whether the deceased shared the materialist or spiritualist doctrine, an orator is chosen professing one or other of those opinions. In the former case, he expands in his funeral oration on the pitiless cruelty of death, which destroys in the blink of an eye the most beautiful intelligences, leaving nothing but a memory, often very fleeting, in the hearts of those who have known us.

If, on the contrary, the preacher chosen is a spiritualist, he speaks about the existence of spirits, their happy or unhappy state, their intervention in the events of life, the means of evoking them and of entering into communication with them, in order to know what has become of them and to ask their advice.

When the funeral oration is finished, the coffin is lifted up, the funeral procession forms up again and heads through the subterranean passages to the railway leading to the cemetery. That railway leaves the International Palace at the extremity of the Île Saint-Louis; it goes along the Quai de l'Arsenal, crosses the Faubourg Saint-Antoine and Saint-Mandé and terminates in the Bois de Vincennes, where it splits into several branches.

It is that wood which serves the Socialists as a cemetery. It has not changed its appearance, however, in spite of its new destination. In fact, the socialist religion, differing in that respect from all other cults, does not erect any tombs to its dead. Trees, grass and flowers are all that one finds in its cemeteries, and one does not even see the slight elevations of the terrain that design the form of the coffin and indicate the places where someone has been interred.

Nothing in such a necropolis is a reminder of the dead, except for tiny epitaphs lost in the long grass, on which the names and professions of the dead are inscribed, with the dates of their birth and death. When one desires to have more information about a dead person, one has only to go into little kiosks, in which one finds registers containing, in chronological order, all the funeral orations of the dead people interred in the vicinity.

Concessions of plots in socialist cemeteries are all equal, measuring two meters by three. They are given gratuitously to every citizen who professes the socialist religion on the day of the ceremony celebrating their majority or abjuration.

Many concessionaries never visit the plot allocated to them, fearing that it might bring bad luck. Others, on the contrary, go there frequently; they put flowers there, plant trees, install seats and make a small garden on the lugubrious spot, in which they like to come to rest. In any case, for those who have no fear of the neighborhood of the dead, there is no park as beautiful as the cemetery of Vincennes and nowhere else that one sees trees with such rich crowns, flowers as bright or grass as green and lush.

## 5. Pleasures

The Parisians, and especially the Parisiennes, of the year 2000, are extremely fond of pleasure. They certainly work assiduously all day, but when evening comes it is absolutely necessary that they seek distraction and amusement. Staying at home is a torture, and, for the benefit of their physical and mental health, they need to go out, to take the air, to go somewhere and see someone. Society is organized to that effect, and one can say that there is no other country in which pleasures are as numerous, as varied and as cheap.

In the first place, merely strolling in the evening in the salon-streets and shop-streets is a fine distraction, which costs nothing. The inhabitants of Paris use it, and abuse it. Men come to watch women passing by, women come to be admired, and the more beautiful half of the population is always occupied in providing a spectacle for the other.

One gets bored with everything, though, even idling. That eventuality has been anticipated, however, and a thousand establishments of pleasure open their doors to strollers.

Firstly, there are immense cafés, luxuriously decorated, brightly lit, and filled with noisy crowds. In these cafes all kinds of games can be played—billiards, cards, dominoes, etc.—and one can buy drinks there; or, to put it more accurately, simulacra of drinks, for the Parisians are the most sober people on Earth. They are served a finger of beer in a magnificently-carved tankard, a spoonful of coffee in a Sèvres cup, a drop of liqueur in a muslin-glass, and that is sufficient for them, their stomach being content as soon as their eyes are satisfied.

The great distraction of Parisians, however—the one for which they forget to eat and drink—consists of spectacles. Those are extremely numerous and of every kind. There are establishments for drama, comedy, vaudeville, opera, singers, dancers, feats of strength and skill, etc. Some of them are also cafés, where one can smoke and drink, but the most highly-appreciated and those that attract the biggest crowds are the "Theater-Journals."

That name is given to theaters where the program changes every evening and is an exact representation or burlesque of the day's events. If, for example, there has been a fire or a murder, since the previous day, the events are reproduced on the stage, with so much fidelity that it is as if one were seeing the reality. On the other hand, when the news or a person in the news that day is amenable to parody, however slightly, they are represented in caricature, in mime or in song, adding burlesque details and absurd reflections, thus composing scenes so hilarious and side-splitting that they excite long burst of inextinguishable laughter in the most morose individuals.

Parisians love these sorts of diversions, and these parodies, far from doing any harm to the citizens who furnish their subject-matter, are, on the contrary, the best guarantee of serious celebrity, for if ridicule kills imbeciles, it puts intelligent people on pedestals.

The French are the most sociable people in the world, and their greatest pleasure, after spectacles, is to come together in soirées.

Every Decadi (see the following section) the Government holds a great official ball in the salons of the International Palace. The salons in question are the most magnificent in the world, genuinely magical in their appearance by virtue of their number, variety and decoration.

Here, there are immense ballrooms, dazzling with gold, mirrors and light, where thousands of couples are dancing to the sounds of a stirring orchestra. There, there is a huge winter-garden, with cool shade and sparkling fountains, where tropical plants display their luxuriant vegetation and fill the atmosphere with the heady scents of the forest.

To the side there are discreet boudoirs, where thick woolen carpets muffle footsteps and where softly-upholstered love-seats invite the prolongation of intimate conversations. Elsewhere, there are flower-filled hothouses spreading forth their thousand odorous bouquets, and, competing in brightness and freshness with the flowers, the artificial ornamentations of the heads and bosoms of women.

Further away, there is a somber grotto, rocky and mossy, where a tinkling stream runs; on advancing beneath the vaults one penetrates into a dark corridor where one can scarcely make out one's path—and one thinks that one has already gone astray when one emerges unexpectedly into a splendid buffet, to which dancers

135

repair in haste when their strength is exhausted, and prepare for further exploits.

All the inhabitants of Paris have the right to see these splendors, and everyone receives two or three invitations every year, but many people do not take advantage of them, preferring to cede their places to young people, for whom dancing is such a great pleasure, and who are never as happy as when they are received in the Nation's salons.

In addition to the great Decadi balls, there is a multitude of small gatherings in the city every evening, supported by the State even though they take place in the homes of individuals. This is how.

Whenever a lady declares that she is willing to host a salon, and if she seems capable of doing it well, the Administration will allow her a certain sum toward the expenses of the occasion. With that money, the ladies in question can obtain more spacious accommodation, procure refreshments and receive their friends and acquaintances.

Nothing could be more various than these kinds of soirées. In some people are serious, talking earnestly about politics and literature and playing whist; in others, women work around a lamp, talking about fabrics and trifles, and playing some social game; in others, people dance, make music, recite verses, enact skits, sing songs or play charades, etc.; finally, in some people smoke, drink punch, laugh or converse noisily, and play games of chance. Everyone chooses the salons to attend that suit their taste and mood, and meet up there with people who share their inclinations.

The Government has a very simple means of ensuring that its funds are well-employed and entrusted to good hands: that is by finding out whether particular salons are well-attended. When one of them is found to be deserted, and respiring ennui, the allocation is withdrawn from the host and given to someone else. To avoid that insult, the hostesses go to any lengths, doing anything they can imagine to attract and retain visitors, and there is an ardent competition between all those charmers—a competition from which the public profits, and which procures citizens agreeable and varied ways to spend their evenings.

## 6. The Calendar, Holidays and National Festivals

The French of the year 2000 have renounced the Catholic calendar and have replaced it with another, known as the Republican calendar, which is much more scientific and convenient.

In this calendar, the year begins at the autumnal equinox. It is divided into twelve equal months of thirty days, the names of which are in accord with the seasons. They are:

Three autumn months: Vendémiaire, the month of vintages; Brumaire, the month of fogs; and Frimaire, the month of frosts;

Three winter months: Nivôse, the month of snows; Pluviose, the month of rains; and Ventôse, the month of winds;

Three spring months: Germinal, the month of germination; Floréal, the month of flowers; and Prairial, the month of grass;

Finally, three summer months: Messidor, the month of crops; Thermidor, the month of heat; and Fructidor, the month of fruits.

At the end of Fructidor there are five so-called "complementary" intercalary days, which are not part of any months and serve to complete the 365 days of the solar year.

Each month is divided into three decades of ten days, and each day bears a name in accord with its numerical order. Thus, the first is called Primidi, the second Duodi, the third Tridi, the fourth Quartidi, the fifth Quintidi, the sixth Sextidi, the seventh Septidi, the eighth Octidi, the ninth Nonidi and the tenth Decadi.

Every day begins at midnight and is divided into two sets of ten hours, one starting at midnight and the other at noon. Every hour is divided into a hundred minutes, or fifty double-minutes, and every minute into a hundred seconds. All the clocks and watches in the country indicate the time according to the new system, which had already been adopted long before for astronomical calculations.

Naturally, the days of the Republican year are no longer dedicated to the saints of the Catholic Church, but to Benefactors of Humankind. The birthdates of all the people who, in one way or another, have rendered service to human kind have been identified, and their names have been inscribed on that same day in the new calendar. As for great men whose birthdate is unknown, they are distributed throughout the year in such a way that every day is dedicated to a near-equal number of individuals. When Socialists baptize their children, they usually give them one of the names inscribed on the day of the birth, so that all citizens bear the name of some benefactor of humankind and have an excellent model for imitation in their patron.

Decadi is the day officially devoted to rest. On that day, the Government gives leave to all its employees and workers, and self-employed individuals, following that example, also rest—but there is no obligation on them to do so, and people who want to work on Decadi are perfectly free to do so.

In certain administrations, where the service cannot be interrupted, such as railways, public transport, the mail, etc., there is no general leave granted on Decadi, but a number of the employees are rested on each day of the decad, and their posts are taken by a brigade of supernumeraries.

A different procedure is followed in retail establishments where the public needs to buy gods on a daily basis; such shops only close for every second Decadi and alternate in remaining open on the other.

Finally, certain establishments, such as theaters, cafes and restaurants, obtain their best receipts on Decadi. Naturally, they do not close on that day, and when their employees take their leave they are replaced by supernumeraries.

Every Quintidi the Government accords a half-holiday to its employees and closes those public administrations whose services are not indispensable at noon. Individuals similarly chose that day to take some rest, with the result that the city the takes on a holiday appearance as pronounced as on Decadi.

This is how the Socialists employ their days of leave.

If the weather is poor, they take a turn around the salon-streets or visit some kind of exhibition, and women take advantage of the circumstance to put on their best clothes and compete in elegance.

In that regard, let us say a few words about the costumes of the Republicans of the year 2000.

Men are uniformly clad in dark colors and equally fine fabrics, so it is impossible to deduce the social situation of strollers from their clothing. However, as many employees are quite determined to let other people know what they are, they put on a regulation cap indicating the administration to which they belong and the rank they occupy therein. Such caps are not obligatory, however, and those who wear them do so by choice.

Moreover, there is no official costume or uniform anywhere in the Republic; the most senior magistrates, the ministers and judges dress like everyone else and seek to impose respect by their personal merit and not by their accoutrements.

Women are much less free than men and are subject to a despotic law that regulates the smallest details of the cut, color and fabric of their garments, the form of their hats and the disposition of their hair, including its color. That tyrannical law, which no woman dares infringe, however independent she might be, is "fashion."

It is difficult to define fashion, but let us try.

Suppose that for some garment, a model has been found combining all the conditions of comfort, cheapness and good taste at the same time. Any other people would conserve it preciously and make use of it all the time—but Parisiennes do not think like that, and as soon as they have perceived that a model in every respect they immediately change it and replace it with another, which is ugly, uncomfortable and expensive. People tire of that new invention very rapidly, and create another, which is no better, and then another, which is even worse, and so on, indefinitely, the thirst for novelty being such that it is necessary to find it at any price, however abominable it might be.

It is that furious rate of change that constitutes fashion. It reigns despotically over the women of Paris, who are its humble and obedient slaves. Thus, it is easy to describe in a single word the costume of the Parisiennes of the ear 2000. They are always rigorously clad in the latest fashion.

But let us get back to the employment citizens make of their holidays.

When the weather is good, they stroll in the boulevards, the Champs-Élysées, the Bois de Boulogne, or even, in the summer, go into the countryside. The Parisians adore the countryside, not as a place to live but as a place to spend a few hours and see something different from the city. Every Decadi, when the weather permits, the population hastens to the railway stations and goes to spend the day in the surrounding fields and forests.

For those who have a few days' holiday there are more distant excursions, pleasure trains to go to the seaside, spa towns, Switzerland, and Alps, the Pyrenees, etc. These pleasure trains operate at reduced prices, and the Government, which owns the hotels where the travelers stay, does not exploit them by charging more for rooms than anywhere else.

Parisians are very fond of these long-distance excursions, and many save up during the year in order that they might undertake brief voyages within France or abroad during their holidays. The desire to see everything and to know everything is the dominant passion of Parisians, and although they know perfectly well that their beloved capital is the nicest place in the world, they leave it gladly, only to find it all the more beautiful when they return.

In addition to the Decadi leave, there are several national festivals in the Republic of the year 2000, on which the Government sets its employees at liberty and the entire population stops work.

Firstly, there is the anniversary of the foundation of the Social Republic, an anniversary that is celebrated with patriotic hymns, appropriate spectacles, regattas, velocipede races,[9] illuminations, fireworks, etc.

Then there is another solemnity, of an entirely different character: the Day of the Dead. On that day, an assembled crowd goes to the cemeteries, carrying flowers and pious souvenirs to those who are no more.

The Republic's greatest national festival, however, is that of the five complementary days. Throughout their duration, all work that is not indispensable is abandoned, and people think about nothing but enjoying themselves. It is the epoch that Parisians have chosen for their carnival, and although it is only five days long, as many follies are committed there as if it lasted for a whole year.

While young people amuse themselves by donning disguises, however, the Government is occupied with more serious matters. In solemn sessions it takes stock of the Republic's affairs during the year that has just elapsed, reading reports on the internal external situation, the actions of the Administration, the progress of Industry and Agriculture, the works of artists and writers, etc.

The last of the complementary days is devoted to the distribution of national rewards. It is the biggest festival of the year, and is celebrated with public rejoicing of unparalleled magnificence, to which the citizens' masquerade communicates an extraordinary animation. All the young and cheerful individuals put on their cos-

---

[9] Although velocipedes (i.e, bicycles) were not really new in 1869, there is a sense in which they were the "latest thing," the innovative addition of pedals to the front wheel of the mass-produced Michaux velocipede provoking a veritable craze on the boulevards of Paris from late 1867 to the outbreak of the Franco-Prussian War.

tumes; all the promenades are packed with floats crowded with masks, splendid corteges or burlesques emblematically representing the work of various industries, or parodying the events of the year, amusing the crowds with their clowning.

In the evening, the Government hosts a great masked ball in the salons of the International Palace; at the same time, in all the theaters, all the dance-halls and even the public squares, other costumed balls are organized, which are not official but are no less merry, and where the masquerades of the corteges come to continue the day's amusements.

At midnight, a salvo of cannon-fire announces the end of the year; the dancers pause in their capers momentarily, and shout: "Long live the Social Republic;" bands strike up the *Marseillaise*, the assembled crowds sing the national hymn—and then the new year is enthusiastically introduced by dancing, and indulging in a thousand follies, until dawn.

# SF & FANTASY

Henri Allorge. *The Great Cataclysm*
Guy d'Armen. *Doc Ardan: The City of Gold and Lepers*
G.-J. Arnaud. *The Ice Company*
Charles Asselineau. *The Double Life*
Cyprien Bérard. *The Vampire Lord Ruthwen*
Aloysius Bertrand. *Gaspard de la Nuit*
Richard Bessière. *The Gardens of the Apocalypse*
Albert Bleunard. *Ever Smaller*
Félix Bodin. *The Novel of the Future*
Louis Boussenard. *Monsieur Synthesis*
Alphonse Brown. *City of Glass; The Conquest of the Air*
André Caroff. *The Terror of Madame Atomos; Miss Atomos; The Return of Madame Atomos; The Mistake of Madame Atomos; The Monsters of Madame Atomos; The Revenge of Madame Atomos*
Félicien Champsaur. *The Human Arrow; Ouha, King of the Apes; Pharaoh's Wife*
Didier de Chousy. *Ignis*
Captain Danrit. *Undersea Odyssey*
C. I. Defontenay. *Star (Psi Cassiopeia)*
Charles Derennes. *The People of the Pole*
Georges Dodds (anthologist). *The Missing Link*
Harry Dickson. *The Heir of Dracula*
Jules Dornay. *Lord Ruthven Begins*
Alfred Driou. *The Adventures of a Parisian Aeronaut*
Sâr Dubnotal *vs. Jack the Ripper*
Alexandre Dumas. *The Return of Lord Ruthven*
Renée Dunan. *Baal*
J.-C. Dunyach. *The Night Orchid; The Thieves of Silence*
Henri Duvernois. *The Man Who Found Himself*
Achille Eyraud. *Voyage to Venus*
Henri Falk. *The Age of Lead*
Paul Féval. *Anne of the Isles; Knightshade; Revenants; Vampire City; The Vampire Countess; The Wandering Jew's Daughter*
Paul Féval, *fils. Felifax, the Tiger-Man*
Charles de Fieux. *Lamékis*
Arnould Galopin. *Doctor Omega; Doctor Omega and the Shadowmen*
Judith Gautier. *Isoline and the Serpent-Flower*

Léon Gozlan. *The Vampire of the Val-de-Grâce*
G.L. Gick. *Harry Dickson and the Werewolf of Rutherford Grange*
Edmond Haraucourt. *Illusions of Immortality*
Nathalie Henneberg. *The Green Gods*
V. Hugo, P. Foucher & P. Meurice. *The Hunchback of Notre-Dame*
Romain d'Huissier. *Hexagon: Dark Matter*
Michel Jeury. *Chronolysis*
Gustave Kahn. *The Tale of Gold and Silence*
Gérard Klein. *The Mote in Time's Eye*
Fernand Kolney. *Love in 5000 Years*
Louis-Guillaume de La Follie. *The Unpretentious Philosopher*
Jean de La Hire. *Enter the Nyctalope; The Nyctalope on Mars; The
Nyctalope vs. Lucifer; The Nyctalope Steps In; Night of the Nyctalope*
Etienne-Léon de Lamothe-Langon. *The Virgin Vampire*
André Laurie. *Spiridon*
Gabriel de Lautrec. *The Vengeance of the Oval Portrait*
Alain le Drimeur. *The Future City*
Georges Le Faure & Henri de Graffigny. *The Extraordinary Adven-
tures of a Russian Scientist Across the Solar System* (2 vols.)
Gustave Le Rouge. *The Vampires of Mars; The Dominion of the
World* (w/Gustave Guitton) (4 vols.)
Jules Lermina. *Mysteryville; Panic in Paris; To-Ho and the Gold
Destroyers; The Secret of Zippelius*
Jean-Marc & Randy Lofficier. *Edgar Allan Poe on Mars; The Katri-
na Protocol; Pacifica; Robonocchio; Tales of the Shadowmen 1-9*
Xavier Mauméjean. *The League of Heroes*
Joseph Méry. *The Tower of Destiny*
Hippolyte Mettais. *The Year 5865*
Louise Michel. *The Human Microbes; The New World*
Tony Moilin. *Paris in the Year 2000*
José Moselli. *Illa's End*
John-Antoine Nau. *Enemy Force*
Marie Nizet. *Captain Vampire*
C. Nodier, A. Beraud & Toussaint-Merle. *Frankenstein*
Henri de Parville. *An Inhabitant of the Planet Mars*
Gaston de Pawlowski. *Journey to the Land of the 4th Dimension*
Georges Pellerin. *The World in 2000 Years*
Ernest Pérochon. *The Frenetic People*
Pierre Pelot. *The Child Who Walked on the Sky*
J. Polidori, C. Nodier, E. Scribe. *Lord Ruthven the Vampire*
P.-A. Ponson du Terrail. *The Vampire and the Devil's Son*

Henri de Régnier. *A Surfeit of Mirrors*
Maurice Renard. *The Blue Peril; Doctor Lerne; The Doctored Man; A Man Among the Microbes; The Master of Light*
Jean Richepin. *The Wing; The Crazy Corner*
Albert Robida. *The Adventures of Saturnin Farandoul; The Clock of the Centuries; Chalet in the Sky*
J.-H. Rosny Aîné. *Helgvor of the Blue River; The Givreuse Enigma; The Mysterious Force; The Navigators of Space; Vamireh; The World of the Variants; The Young Vampire*
Marcel Rouff. *Journey to the Inverted World*
Han Ryner. *The Superhumans*
Brian Stableford. *The New Faust at the Tragicomique; The Empire of the Necromancers (The Shadow of Frankenstein; Frankenstein and the Vampire Countess; Frankenstein in London); Sherlock Holmes & The Vampires of Eternity; The Stones of Camelot; The Wayward Muse.* (anthologist) *The Germans on Venus; News from the Moon; The Supreme Progress; The World Above the World; Nemoville; Investigations of the Future*
Jacques Spitz. *The Eye of Purgatory*
Kurt Steiner. *Ortog*
Eugène Thébault. *Radio-Terror*
C.-F. Tiphaigne de La Roche. *Amilec*
Théo Varlet. *The Golden Rock. The Xenobiotic Invasion; Timeslip Troopers* (w/André Blandin); *The Martian Epic* (w/Octave Joncquel)
Paul Vibert. *The Mysterious Fluid*
Villiers de l'Isle-Adam. *The Scaffold; The Vampire Soul*
Philippe Ward. *Artahe*
Philippe Ward & Sylvie Miller. *The Song of Montségur*

## MYSTERIES & THRILLERS

M. Allain & P. Souvestre. *The Daughter of Fantômas*
A. Anicet-Bourgeois, Lucien Dabril. *Rocambole*
A. Bernède. *Belphegor*; *Judex* (w/Louis Feuillade); *The Return of Judex* (w/Louis Feuillade)
A. Bisson & G. Livet. *Nick Carter vs. Fantômas*
V. Darlay & H. de Gorsse. *Arsène Lupin vs. Sherlock Holmes: The Stage Play*
Séamas Duffy. *Sherlock Holmes in Paris*
Paul Féval. *Gentlemen of the Night; John Devil; The Black Coats ('Salem Street; The Invisible Weapon; The Parisian Jungle; The*

*Companions of the Treasure; Heart of Steel; The Cadet Gang; The Sword-Swallower)*

Emile Gaboriau. *Monsieur Lecoq*

Goron & Emile Gautier. *Spawn of the Penitentiary*

Steve Leadley. *Sherlock Holmes: The Circle of Blood*

Maurice Leblanc. *Arsène Lupin vs. Countess Cagliostro; Arsène Lupin vs. Sherlock Holmes (The Blonde Phantom; The Hollow Needle); The Many Faces of Arsène Lupin*

Gaston Leroux. *Chéri-Bibi; The Phantom of the Opera; Rouletabille & the Mystery of the Yellow Room; Rouletabille at Krupp's*

Richard Marsh. *The Complete Adventures of Judith Lee*

William Patrick Maynard. *The Terror of Fu Manchu; The Destiny of Fu Manchu*

Frank J. Morlock. *Sherlock Holmes: The Grand Horizontals; Sherlock Holmes vs Jack the Ripper*

Antonin Reschal. *The Adventures of Miss Boston*

P. de Wattyne & Y. Walter. *Sherlock Holmes vs. Fantômas*

David White. *Fantômas in America*

## SCREENPLAYS

Mike Baron. *The Iron Triangle*

Emma Bull & Will Shetterly. *Nightspeeder; War for the Oaks*

Gerry Conway & Roy Thomas. *Doc Dynamo*

Steve Englehart. *Majorca*

James Hudnall. *The Devastator*

Jean-Marc & Randy Lofficier. *Royal Flush*

J.-M. & R. Lofficier & Marc Agapit. *Despair*

J.-M. & R. Lofficier & Joël Houssin. *City*

Andrew Paquette. *Peripheral Vision*

Robert L. Robinson, Jr. *Judex*

R. Thomas, J. Hendler & L. Sprague de Camp. *Rivers of Time*

## NON-FICTION

Stephen R. Bissette. *Blur 1-5. Green Mountain Cinema 1; Teen Angels*

Win Scott Eckert. *Crossovers* (2 vols.)

Jean-Marc & Randy Lofficier. *Shadowmen* (2 vols.)

Randy Lofficier. *Over Here*

## ART BOOKS

Jean-Pierre Normand. *Science Fiction Illustrations*
Raven Okeefe. *Raven's L'il Critters; Rave's Faves*
Randy Lofficier & Raven Okeefe. *If Your Possum Go Daylight...*
Daniele Serra. *Illusions*

## HEXAGON COMICS

Franco Frescura & Luciano Bernasconi. *Wampus*
Franco Frescura & Giorgio Trevisan. *CLASH*
L. Bernasconi, J.-M. Lofficier & Juan Roncagliolo Berger. *Phenix*
Claude Legrand, J.-M. Lofficier & L. Bernasconi. *Kabur*
Franco Oneta. *Zembla*
L. Buffolente, Lofficier & J.-J. Dzialowski. *Strangers: Homicron*
Danilo Grossi. *Strangers: Jaydee*
Claude Legrand & Luciano Bernasconi. *Strangers: Starlock*